Spy Flash

A Collection of Espionage Flash Fiction

P. A. DUNCAN

Cover Design: SelfPubBookCovers.com/Snowmoondesigns

ISBN: 0985524812
ISBN-13: 978-0985524814

DEDICATION

To those who have died in covert service to their countries and whose names we will never know.

EPIGRAPH

"We give thanks to the countless intelligence and counterterrorism professionals who've worked tirelessly to achieve this outcome. The American people do not see their work, nor know their names. But tonight, they feel the satisfaction of their work and the result of their pursuit of justice."

--President Barack Obama, May 2, 2011
Announcing the death of Osama Bin Laden

CONTENTS

ACKNOWLEDGEMENTS

My thanks for the encouragement from my fellow workshoppers at the Tinker Mountain Writers Workshop, my wonderful writers group, SWAG Writers, and especially Jennie Coughlin. Without her Rory's Story Cube Challenge, there'd be no Spy Flash.

Finally, thanks to David McCallum and Robert Vaughn for inspiration.

CAST OF CHARACTERS

Alexei N. Bukharin – Defection from the Soviet Union, top operative for the United Nations Intelligence Directorate.

Maitland "Mai" Fisher – English aristocrat, recruited as a teenager because her late parents were Directorate operatives, Bukharin's partner.

Nigel Hume – First operational head of the United Nations Intelligence Directorate.

Nelson – prefers to go by one name, Bukharin's former partner, Hume's successor.

John Stone – Head of the London Directorate Station, worked with Mai Fisher's parents, recruited Mai Fisher.

Edwin Terrell, Jr. – CIA field operative (sometimes called a case manager), worked on occasion with Alexei and Nelson and now Alexei and Mai.

United Nations Intelligence Directorate – aka The Directorate, the intelligence arm of the United Nations; can be called on by any signatory to its charter to supply "neutral" intelligence; its operational head can also use operatives at his discretion without the knowledge of a signatory. Officially, The Directorate does not exist.

- 1 -

DESERT NIGHTS AND WEEPING FLOWERS

Egypt, 1964

Alexei Bukharin thought the setting a cliché: a half-moon, the desert outside Cairo, the looming shadow of the pyramids of Giza as a backdrop. Even the requisite Egyptian in a *dishdasha* waited.

He stayed in the shadow of a rusting hulk of a bus that tourists trusted to get them here safely. His eyes scanned as he turned 360 degrees around his position. The scant moonlight was enough for him to see he was alone, except for the robed man who watched at the entrance to the smallest of the pyramids on the Giza plateau.

He waited another full hour to assure no one had followed him and emerged from the shadow of the bus, clad in his own version of desert robes, hood up to cover the blond hair that would be a beacon in the moonlight. Though he could get to his gun beneath the robes, his hand lay on the combat knife he'd carried in the Soviet Army. Knives were quieter anyway; guns brought too much unwanted attention. This meet had been well-planned, vetted down to the commas and periods, but he never took chances.

The Egyptian's face broke into a smile when Alexei approached. A hand over his heart, he bowed to Alexei and murmured in Arabic. Alexei caught only a few words—the man you want is there. The Egyptian pointed toward the entrance to the tomb. A faint glow came from within, and Alexei almost shook his head at the deepening of the cliché.

Alexei motioned for the Egyptian to precede him, not wanting the man at his back, and they entered the tomb. Alexei had to hunch to keep from scraping his head on the ceiling of the passageway, but the Egyptian had no such issue.

1

They homed in on the faint glow, and it brightened until they emerged into a square chamber lit with torches. *Boizhe moi*, Alexei thought, *can it get more B movie than this?*

Keeping the exit accessible and his back to a wall of the chamber, Alexei scanned his new surroundings. On a camp table lay the tools of an archeologist—a magnifying glass, a flashlight, picks, brushes, a notebook, colored pencils, a folding ruler. The implements were closest to a wall filled with hieroglyphs and a mural of the life of the Egyptian buried here, he supposed. Alexei could see a decent sketch of the mural on the pages of the open notebook. All that added up to the cover of the person he was supposed to meet.

His hand went back to the hilt of his knife when he heard murmuring—a man's voice, gentle, a woman's soft weeping. From a side chamber two people emerged. A dark-haired man about Alexei's height had his arm around the shoulders of a woman whose robe covered colorful, silken skirts. Alexei could hear the jangle of tiny bells in time with her steps. The woman's head came up when she sensed other people in the room, and Alexei saw her beauty, her eyes rimmed with kohl, which had streaked her cheeks as she wept.

The man carried a pith helmet and wore archeologist chic—jodhpurs, a safari jacket, unbuttoned to show a well-developed chest beneath it, and soft, leather knee boots. The man's rumpled hair looked as if the woman had run her hands through it. Indeed, Alexei could see the remnants of the berry stain the woman used on her lips on the man's mouth.

With a forlorn look at Alexei, the woman dashed across the chamber to the Egyptian and wept onto his shoulder. He soothed her, and they left.

The two men studied each other. Where Alexei's expression was closed and stern, the other man smiled, his brown eyes shining in the torchlight. He lay his helmet on the camp table, took a handkerchief from a pocket of the jacket, and wiped his mouth. The handkerchief went back into the pocket, and he buttoned up the jacket, his eyes never leaving Alexei. A half-smile stayed on his lips.

Alexei cleared his throat and said, "The Yankees' prospects are good this year."

The man laughed and shook his head. "Why is it the code phrases are always baseball-related? I'm more of a football fan myself."

Alexei said nothing, but he drew the knife a half-inch from its sheath.

"Oh, of course," the man said. "Sorry. It's just this is all so trite." His face took on a false seriousness, then he said, "Actually, I think the Red Sox may break the curse of the Bambino this season."

Alexei let the knife slide back into the sheath but kept his hand resting on the hilt. "I am Alexei N. Bukharin. KGB."

"Yeah, you seem to match the picture in your dossier, but, you know, to make a sure identification…" The man pointed to the hood of Alexei's robe, and Alexei pushed it back. A grin came to the man's face again, and he stepped closer, right hand extended.

"Nelson," he said. "United Nations."

Alexei shook the offered hand. "A pleasure to meet you, Mr. Nelson."

"Just Nelson. So, Alex, here we are."

"Please. Alexei, not Alex."

"Of course. Sorry. I have to ask you a few questions."

"I would do the same if you were defecting to the KGB."

Nelson laughed. "That's not too likely, my friend, but I'm glad you understand. This is going to be a complicated relationship. You're defecting from the KGB, which is what they want us to believe, but you're really their mole, which is what they believe, but your defection is real, which is what they don't know."

"We Russians have a history of being obtuse."

"I was born in Ukraine, which is a Soviet Socialist Republic. I was born a Russian, schooled a Russian, but I consider myself Ukrainian."

"You have family in the U.S.S.R. Is that going to be a problem?"

"They will denounce me to the Party, but they are aware of the convoluted situation. They will be no problem."

"Not even the son you left behind?"

Alexei felt heat rise to his face. He thought his mentor had covered that knowledge, but apparently the U.N.'s spy service had resources he—or the KGB—didn't know.

"He's not yet two," Alexei said. "He'll be raised to think I'm dead, like his mother."

Nelson nodded, his eyes narrowing. "Why did you pick us?"

"The U.N. Intelligence Directorate?"

Nelson nodded again, arms folded across his chest.

"If I went to the CIA with this proposal, they would give me a new name and put me in Podunk, America, after debriefing me. I want to fight back against the KGB. I want to bring down the Communist Party."

"Yeah, your little cabal—what's it called again?"

"*Kracniyi Krug.* The Red Circle."

"Right. Well, they have an intriguing plan, but it could take years. You understand that?"

"Of course. Russians are a patient people. If it takes decades, it will." Alexei gave a very Russian shrug, the one where you indicated acceptance of what fate had in store for you.

In Russian, Nelson began, "*Chto yest…*"

"*Yest,*" Alexei finished. What is, is.

3

"All right, that's settled," Nelson said. "Welcome to the United Nations Intelligence Directorate—after we debrief you, of course. Oh, and the pay's not bad, either."

"I'll count money later. Now, it would be bad luck. Why was the woman crying?" Alexei asked.

Nelson seemed nonplussed at the question but recovered, the characteristic grin returning. "She was sad to see me go," he said. "Poor thing. You spend a few days with them, and they think it's for life. She thought the dashing, rich archeologist was going to take her back to America with him. I had to disabuse her of that, naturally."

"Naturally."

"However, because she dances at a lot of diplomatic events, she told me quite a few juicy items that I'll take back to our analysts."

"Pillow talk. Old KGB method."

"Whatever works, my friend. I think you'll find we're a little more flexible than the CIA when it comes to using sex to get information."

Nelson bent down to a small valise leaning against the camp table, but he caught Alexei's hand tightening on his knife again.

"Easy, old man," Nelson said. "A little something for us to seal the deal."

He took out an iced bottle of vodka and two glasses and poured liquid into both. He took up one and handed the other to Alexei.

The two men raised the glasses in a toast.

"Here's..." Nelson paused, gave that open smile again. "Here's to the beginning of a beautiful friendship."

Alexei rolled his eyes. "How did I know you were going to say that?"

They drank and smashed the glasses against the mural.

- 2 -

FOOTSTEPS

London, 1973

Sir John Nevis Stone, GBE, stared at his fifteen-year-old ward and shook his head. The scrubbing he'd ordered had removed the overdone make-up and the dye from her hair. The black jeans, studded leather jacket, and chains were gone, and in her riding pants and casual sweater, she looked more like who she was—the daughter of decent people who gave their lives for an ideal. Still, with her legs crossed at the knee, top leg swinging, the arms folded over her chest, her gaze at some point in the room other than his face, she sat before him, a sullen and defiant adolescent.

The library of her London home wasn't as extensive as the one in the home on her country estate, but it leant this conversation the proper, serious atmosphere.

"Were you listening to me?" he asked her.

That almost got an eye-roll, but she answered, "Yes. I was irresponsible, blah, blah. I wasn't thinking, blah, blah. All the same things you've said since you dragged me away from Amsterdam," Maitland Fisher replied.

"Maitland, really, you make it sound like I kidnapped you. I dragged you out of a drug-sodden rock star's bed, and I'm still considering exactly what I'm going to do about the bastard," Stone said.

She finally made eye contact with him, her face showing her fear, her eyes pleading with him.

"John, please, don't do anything to Ian. I told him I was eighteen. It's not his fault," she said.

"No, my dear, it is his fault, because he shouldn't have taken your word for it. For the meantime, anyway, I'm doing nothing, but if you have any contact—a letter, a post card, a phone call, anything—I'll make certain the media learn about his defilement of an underage girl. Am I clear?"

She sat up in the chair, both feet on the floor, hands gripping the chair arms. "John, he didn't defile me. I wanted…"

"Am I clear?"

She slouched in the chair again. "Yes," she muttered; he strained to hear her.

"Excellent. I'm glad we understand each other. Now," he said, reaching to open a drawer in the desk, "I have something you will read. Once you're finished, we'll discuss your future."

Stone placed two, thick file folders on the desk.

"What are those?" she asked, but he saw her eyes scan the U.N. globe and the red words in a diagonal slash across the cover—Top Secret.

"Information on your parents," he replied.

"My parents were missionaries. Why would the United Nations have Top Secret folders on them?"

"Read them and find out."

She picked up the top one, which happened to be her mother's. "What does the black square mean?" she asked him.

"It means they died in the line of duty."

Her eyes contacted his again, wariness now in them. "They died in a plane crash," she said.

"Did they? Read and find out."

Stone leaned back in his chair and tented his fingers as he watched her open the folder. After a few seconds of reading, she closed it again, and she looked up at him.

"Am I supposed to be seeing this?" she asked.

"Technically, no, but I'm the boss so I have some leeway. Read."

A half-hour passed before she finished and tossed the folders on the desk with such force they slid across the top toward him.

"Those are lies," she said.

"No," he replied. "That's the truth about your parents."

"My parents weren't the kind of people who peek through keyholes and spy on everyone." Her chin came up, defiant, and, damn, but didn't she look like her mother when she did that?

"They were exactly that 'kind of people,' and now that you know, you have some thinking to do."

"About what?"

"I want you to finish their work."

"What? Why?"

"Because given your recent behavior, they'd be ashamed to call you their daughter, and you have to do something to restore their honor, which you've dragged through layers of mud."

He intended his words to sting, and they did. The girl began to weep, her head lowered, and he steeled himself to be unaffected by it.

"Now," he said, "you can go be the idle aristocrat you claim to abhor. You can go to the right parties, marry the right lesser lord, who'll be more than willing to count your money for you, and give him a brace of children destined to make nothing of their lives either. Or you can follow in the footsteps of two very brave people who wanted only to make a better world."

She raised her head, fingers swiping at the tears on her cheeks. "You make it sound so noble. Digging dirt on people and worse," she said. "Why did you lie to me for so long?"

"Maitland, you were five when they were murdered. You could understand a plane crash, not that your parents were spies, burned by someone they trusted, and killed by a foreign government," he said. He saw her wince and added, "I did what I thought was best. I never planned on being a father, but there I was, responsible for a five-year-old child while trying to run a covert organization and keep that from you."

"So, you're not MI-5?"

"No, this is a U.N. organization, but there'll be more time to explain all that later. I need your answer."

"Right now?"

"Yes."

"Well, I think it's a horrible idea."

"I didn't ask your opinion. I want your answer."

He watched her rise and walk to the fireplace, where she stared for a while at the flames before her eyes came up to a framed picture on the mantelpiece—Katherine Maitland and Lord Frederick Fisher on their wedding day with their witness, merely plain John Stone then.

"They don't look like spies," she said.

Stone crossed the room to her. "No, they look like who they were, two people very much in love getting married. That love was what orphaned you. Your mother wasn't the type to stay home and pace the floor waiting for your father to get back from a mission. That's why she switched from cryptography to operations during the war. That's why when he and I joined The Directorate, she came, too, as his partner."

"So, I was nothing to them, that they left me so often."

"No, dear girl, you were everything to them. As I said, it may sound like a cliché, but they wanted a better world for you."

"What happened to the person who… What was the word?"

"Who burned them?" She nodded. "She was their translator for many years on Taiwan, but the government there began to suspect she was a Communist. She gave your parents up to save her life, but the authorities killed her anyway."

"Well, that's some solace." Maitland turned to him. "What makes you think I can do this?"

"Because you are their daughter. You are your mother's daughter."

"Would they want me to do this?"

"Lord, no! I suspect they'll haunt me for even suggesting this, but I don't want you to think about that. I'm giving you a chance to finish their work."

Her eyes narrowed at him. "If you don't let me see Ian Flynn again, I'll go to the press and tell them all about this super-secret Directorate," she said.

"No, you won't."

"Won't I?"

"No, because you're your parents' child. Faced with death they kept their oath. A lot to live up to, to be sure, but you can do it. In fact, that little threat proved it to me. You've got what it takes."

For a moment he thought he'd get slapped, but she glanced once more at her parents' picture and back at the fire. When she looked at him again, it was her mother who stood there, the woman who'd been the best covert operative he'd ever encountered, male or female, and John Stone felt a rare qualm that he would lose the innocent girl Maitland had been, much as he'd lost her mother to Freddie Fisher thirty years before.

"Where do I start?" she asked.

- 3 -

FAMILY MATTERS

London, 1976

When Mai entered the conference room, she smiled at John Stone, and she saw MacArthur Holt. She gave him a smile as well and got his usual scowl in return. He was an Eton man, reaching for a title, but John had confidence in him. His field work had diminished as Stone had involved him more in management.

Mai thought he had a bit of a James Bond streak. Holt wore only the best suits, carried a Walther PPK in a shoulder holster, and had a fondness for martinis. She often wondered if he took them shaken, not stirred. Today, he wore an immaculate white shirt and striped tie, the shoulder holster over the shirt but daring not to wrinkle it. He stood by the window, hands on hips.

"You wanted to see me?" she said to John.

"Yes, Mai. Sit down," John said, an off-hand smile showing.

Her stomach lurched, and she wondered if she'd done something wrong. No, she thought, the last dead drop went exactly as intended. She sat at the table as John took his seat at the head.

Holt sat across from her, arms on the tabletop, fingers interlaced. If anything, the scowl deepened.

"Is this about the dead drop in Rome?" she asked John.

"No, not at all. That went well. We debriefed that. Excellent work. This is the next step."

"The next step to what?" she asked.

"You expect to fill and clear dead drops and eavesdrop at society parties your entire career?" Holt asked, his derision unconcealed.

"I'm sorry, Arthur," she said, "have I done something to upset you?"

"No, Mai," Stone said. "Arthur is upset that I assigned him to work you through a new project."

"John, I'm not upset," Holt said. "Rather, I think I should be working with someone a bit more experienced."

"Arthur, how will she get experience except through tutelage from an experienced agent?"

"I'd prefer she have a few more ops under her belt."

"'She' is sitting here and has never liked it when others discuss her in the third person in front of her," Mai said.

"Easy, old girl," John said. "Arthur, get started with the briefing."

Holt opened a folder that had been at his right hand, took out a picture, and slid it across the table toward her. She picked it up and studied it, getting a vague memory of a man with a younger face in a corner of a pub, playing a guitar and singing Irish songs. Holt passed her the file, which she began to read.

"Fintan Maitland," she said and looked up at Holt.

"You should know him. He's your cousin," Holt said.

"His father and my grandfather were siblings. That makes him my mother's first cousin, mine once removed or some such. I don't think I've seen him since I was eight or nine."

"You don't think?" Holt asked.

"Excuse me?"

"He's your cousin."

"Yes, we've established that. I think the last time I saw him was during a summer visit to a family house in Belfast when I was eight or nine. He was singing at a local pub."

"And there's been no contact with you since?" Holt asked.

"No, but he may have had 'contact,' as you call it, with Roisin O'Saidh. She manages the money of anyone who was left funds from my mother's estate," Mai replied.

"Mr. Maitland has indeed 'spoken with' Miss O'Saidh about money recently. She denied him."

"I'm sure she had her reasons," Mai said. Roisin had cut her off often enough.

"Those reasons were probably that any money he gets he funnels to the IRA," Holt said, with a smirk.

"There have been factions of the Maitland family with connections to the IRA," Mai said. "John is aware of that. John, I thought you said something about a next step. This feels like an interrogation."

"I was beginning to notice that. Arthur, shall we get to the point?" Stone asked.

Holt was not happy to be brought back on topic. He gave Stone a glare, and turned it again on Mai. "All right, then. The 'next step' John is talking about is recruiting. You're going to recruit Fintan Maitland to provide us information on the IRA."

"Which you'll, in turn, provide to MI-5."

"You have a problem with that?"

"No. I wanted to be clear about that fact if I'm supposed to betray a part of my family."

Holt smiled for the first time, though it had some inner triumph behind it. "This is the profession you've said you wanted, following in Mummy and Daddy's footsteps, and all that. Part of this profession is betrayal, and sometimes you betray friends, family, whatever it takes. If you have qualms, tell us now, and you can go back to the Army or the RAF." Mai looked at John Stone, whose face was utterly neutral. "No, don't look at him! This op is you and me."

"Maybe the op should involve only you," Mai said.

"Arthur, give us a moment," Stone said.

"John, I…"

"A moment, Arthur," John repeated, giving him a pointed look.

Holt stood up and shoved the chair back under the table before stalking from the room and slamming the door.

"God, who squeezed his balls?" Mai said.

"Mai," Stone said, his voice so sharp, she jumped. "This is not a business where you get to pick and choose what you do or with whom you work, and you do not play on our relationship."

"When did I do that?" she asked, genuinely surprised.

"Calling on me when Arthur's questions got too pointed, looking to me to intercede when it gets too hard on you."

"But I…"

"I'm talking now as your superior, not your lover. Understand?"

"Of course."

"You will recruit Fintan Maitland, and you will do it under Arthur's supervision. You will do exactly what he says, when he says. If you do not recruit Fintan, you're finished. Do you understand?"

She swallowed the lump in her throat and fought tears. "You've never spoken to me that way."

"Don't put me in a situation where I have to."

"Why can't you supervise me on this, like the dead drops?"

"Mai, I supervise thirty full-time agents, manage the budget, provide logistics for four satellite offices, deal with agencies from every European government and America. I don't have the time to oversee a trainee. And this is a test for Arthur. He wants to transition to management."

"So I'm the guinea pig?"

"Have you changed your mind about becoming a full operative?"

"No, of course not."

"Get it through your head that you don't get to plan out your career here yet. You'll work with Arthur on this mission, and I better get a good report from him."

Before she could stop them, the tears spilled over her cheeks. She swiped them away and tried to keep more from falling.

"I'm going to get Arthur," Stone said, rising. "Get yourself straightened out. I don't want him to see you crying."

Stone left her alone after tossing her his handkerchief, and she fought her emotions, trying to get them under control. She wasn't certain why she was so emotional about this. She barely knew Fintan, but she didn't understand why Holt was so dead set against her.

Not for the first time, she questioned her choice, but one thing she never did was quit, despite both the Army and RAF thinking that was the case. She did those things to make certain she'd never cower in a hotel closet again after a blown dead drop.

Using the handkerchief, and her reflection in the window, she made herself presentable right before the door opened and Holt returned—alone.

"All right, then," he said. "Are you on board?"

"Of course."

"Sit down."

"Look, Arthur, John read me the riot act, and I understand the roles, but ordering me about isn't going to do either of us any good."

"Apparently, you weren't listening when Stone said you were finished here if you didn't recruit Fin Maitland."

"Oh, I fully intend to do that, but keep pushing me, and I'll do exactly opposite of what you want. Meaning you don't get your shot at management either."

For a moment she thought she'd overstepped and that Holt would throttle her, but he laughed and shook his head.

"You've learned the manipulation lesson very well," he commented. "I'm glad we understand each other. You want to make the grade and so do I."

He gestured to a chair, and she sat. He sat down, an empty chair between them. "Tell me what you remember about Fintan Maitland." He looked at her, smirked, and added, "If you please."

She decided that was bait, and she wouldn't rise to it. "What I said earlier sums it up. I was visiting the Belfast cousins, and he was playing guitar and singing at a local pub. He had a beard then."

"Did you converse with him?"

"I really don't remember. I'm sure someone introduced us. We were all cousins there, so someone probably did."

"Would he know you're the main heir?"

"I don't know. Probably, if he had some money coming from my mother's estate."

"So, how do you think he'd react to a call from you?"

"I honestly don't know, but if he went to Roisin for money and she refused him, he might think he could get money out of me."

"He's nine years older than you."

"Yes, he was an older teen when I saw him in the pub."

"You find him attractive, attractive enough to sleep with?"

"Jesus Wept, he's my cousin, so, no, I won't be sleeping with him."

Holt smiled again. "What if I tell you to?"

"I'll tell you to do it yourself."

"I'm definitely not his type. He's no wanker."

"I won't work that way. Not for you. Not even for John."

"All right. Here's what you have to do. Make contact with him. Make friends with him. Let him believe you're sympathetic to the IRA, and let it go from there. You'll be wired to get his words to use against him. When he thinks you're going to hand over some money, you play his words back, and tell him the tape is going to MI-5 unless he gives us intelligence on his contacts within the IRA."

"You do know what the IRA do to traitors?"

"Quite well. To make certain you don't have family blood on your hands, you'll have to be careful. So will he."

"Thank youse very much for the fine reception. We'll be passing the hat, so youse be generous."

The applause went on for a few seconds, and he acknowledged it as he put his guitar away in its case. As he wended his way to the bar, patrons called to him, he shook hands, and made brief conversation. At the bar before he could order, the publican put a Guinness in front of him.

"She bought it for you," the publican said and nodded to a woman, a girl really, seated a few stools down.

Fintan Maitland took the glass, lifted it toward her, and took a long draught as he studied her. She could be eighteen or fifteen, so it was best to steer away. Something about her eyes struck a chord with him, and he moved down to the stool next to hers.

She smiled broadly at him, and that seemed familiar, too. He took in the long, chestnut hair, the eyes again.

"Hi, Fin," she said. "I'll wager you don't remember me."

There was no Irish to her voice, only high-brow English, and it all came together. "Jesus Wept, child, but you look like your mother. Come here and give us a hug."

He made certain the hug was loose and brief, the kiss only on her cheek. He hitched a buttock on the stool and drank from his Guinness again. "Well, then, you grew up, you did."

"It happens."

"Little Maitland Fisher. How did you happen to be here?"

"Actually, I call myself Mai now, and I'm looking up my cousin. I did a stint in the Army and the RAF, following in the pater's footsteps, and now I'm looking to have a little fun."

"The Army and the RAF? Mai, you can't be more than seventeen."

"Eighteen, actually. I wanted to get it over with and move on to living, as I said. I remembered you from one summer in Belfast, so I tracked you down."

"How'd you do that, then?"

"Roisin O'Saidh told me you'd come to her for money, and she didn't give you any."

Fin's face screwed into a scowl. "Those O'Saidh's. You'd think the money was theirs."

"Believe me, she keeps it from me, too. Puts me on an allowance," Mai said. "Though, it's a generous allowance, but the damned credit card has a limit, of all things. Anyway, I wanted to look you up. I remembered all those wonderful old songs you sang in Belfast, and I wanted to hear them again."

Fin chuckled a little. "There was a right large group of Protestant boys waiting outside that pub, complaining about those songs. Me and my mates had to run to beat the band to get away from them. Fortunately, we knew the neighborhood better."

She laughed with him, her eyes shining. "Those songs. I've played them over and over."

"They're only songs, Mai."

"They're history."

"Aye, to some. To some, they're old songs about a dead cause, and, me darlin', that's a far too depressing topic to be discussing." He drained his Guinness and stood up. "I appreciate seeing family again, Mai. I'll be playing here for the next week if you care to come back and hear those songs you like. But I need to go get me beauty rest."

"How about I buy you lunch tomorrow?" she said, her hand on his arm.

"Look, love, we're cousins, and I don't rob cradles."

She actually blushed at that. "I'm sorry, Fin. I didn't mean it that way. There's none of my father's family left, and the Maitlands are fewer and fewer every year. I'm looking to reconnect with family. My father didn't want me brought up here, and I want to know my country."

She looked about to cry, and that touched him. "All right, lunch it is," he said. "Though could we make it a late lunch?"

"How about 2 p.m. at Chapter One?" she asked.

"Perfect. I'll see you then, lass."

He kissed her on the cheek again and went to retrieve his guitar. At the door, he turned back and waved to her.

Mai stayed to finish her Guinness, fending off the attentions of an American tourist, and took a cab back to the hotel.

MacArthur Holt waited in her room and that annoyed her. "Your room is next door," she said.

"I wanted to go over the meet with you. The play on family was a good approach."

"Irish men are notoriously sentimental about family. What did you make of the 'dead cause' remark?"

"Are you thinking he's innocent? We have proof of his turning over a lot more money than he could possibly make with his performing to a man we know is an IRA logistician. He's being cautious. You may be long, lost family, but he's been trained not to grab the bait so soon."

"Bait," Mai echoed, feeling something weigh on her.

"Yes, I thought you understood that."

"I feel more like Judas. Arthur, please, I reek of spilled beer and cigarette smoke. I'd like to take a bath and count my thirty pieces of silver."

"You're quite the dramatic, you know."

"Comes with the class, Arthur. Good night, please."

"Of course. We'll discuss how to approach tomorrow's meet in the morning. Rest well."

The bath relaxed her, but she tossed and turned most of the night.

"You bitch!" Fintan Maitland spat at her. "All the talk about the cause, about family, and all the time you're the fooking traitor."

Mai felt her stomach lurch, and she swallowed bile before she spoke. "It's family I'm thinking about, Fin. I'm not letting you stain our name with what you're doing."

"'Our name?' Your name is Fisher, like the English cunt you are."

"And who's the heir and who's not, Fin?"

"Bitch."

"How unoriginal. I have you, on tape, explaining to me that you carry money for the IRA and asking me for money to give the IRA. So, now, I've put you at a fork in the road, Fin. I can turn the tapes over to Home Office, and you end up in H Block, Long Kesh—The Maze."

"I know what it's fooking called."

"Or I can hold onto them, and you give me information."

"I give you information, and you know what they'll fooking do to me?"

"You want me to describe it?"

"Bitch. Cold-hearted bitch."

"Do you really want to roll the die on this, Fin? The ones already in the Maze, they'll kill you when you get there because you got caught. You give me information, and you get to continue exactly what you're doing now. Pass the blood money along."

"I don't expect you to understand. You grew up among the enemy. Big estate. Horses. Cars. Tutors. The IRA protect us from the likes of you."

"The IRA kill innocent people as collateral damage when they go for their military targets. They do more harm to 'the cause' than good. You haven't answered my question."

"The choice you offer is no choice. It's fooking blackmail. You're a fooking blackmailer, and you set me up."

"I didn't make you pass money to the IRA, Fin. You chose to do that. Now, you have another choice. You need to tell me which it is."

"Fooking traitor, English bitch." Fin spat on her.

How she kept from sobbing, she didn't know, but she calmly reached up and wiped his spittle from her cheek. "I guess it's Home Office, then. Say hello to the boys in H Block for me." She got up from the table in his tiny apartment and picked up her jacket. She'd failed. No recruitment, no career.

"Wait, damn it, hold on," Fintan said to her back. "I don't want to go to The Maze."

Before she turned around, she closed her eyes in relief. "Now, you're making sense," she said, but she mouthed to him, "Keep talking."

He frowned at her, but said, "What choice do I have?"

She took a pad and pen from her purse and wrote, "I'll set you up in America."

She said, "You've made the right choice, Fin. It may not seem like it now, but you have."

He took the pen and paper from her and wrote, "Your word?"

"I hope so, but you're still a bitch for how you did this," he told her.

Mai wrote, "My word as a Maitland."

"Maybe, Fin, but you've still done the right thing," she said.

"I'll get you details later," she wrote, showed him, and quietly tore the page from the pad, folded the page, and tucked it in her bra.

"So, how does this work?" Fin asked.

"You come with me, and some people will talk to you."

"Home Office blokes?"

"No. Someone else. Home Office will get the information, but they'll be told it's from a confidential informant. You go on passing the money, but each time you'll tell who gave it to you, who you give it to, how much, when the next money drop is, and so on."

"And you don't think they won't be watching me?"

"You'll have to be careful, won't you? Get your coat. Let's go."

"What, we're doing this now?"

"Yes."

"I have a gig tonight."

"You've already called in with a bad case of laryngitis."

Fin stood up, handsome face contorted in anger, as he kicked over his chair. "Your mother, what would she think of you?" he asked her in Gaelic.

"Don't you ever bring up my mother again, Fintan Maitland," Mai answered him in the same language. "Do it, and I'll give you over to Home Office myself and personally turn the key on your cell in Long Kesh. Do you understand?"

"Yeah, I think I do, *Lady* Fisher."

Mai stood at the window of her hotel and watched a weak moon flee before the dawn. The Dublin skyline was not as familiar to her as it should be. As she'd grown older, she'd become aware of the pitched battle between Roisin O'Saidh and John Stone over her direction in life. It appeared John Stone had won.

MacArthur Holt tapped on the door joining the two rooms and opened it. "He's singing like a drunken Irishman, which is exactly what he is," Arthur said.

"Arthur, I don't find that amusing." She corralled her emotions before she turned to him. He offered no apology.

"At the end, you spoke in, what, Gaelic?" Arthur asked.

"Yes."

"What did he say?"

"Something too nasty for English," she replied. "So, do I have my first recruit?"

"Indeed you do. Congratulations. I didn't think you'd pull it off, you know."

"Yeah, I figured that. Any reason why we can't go back to London, now?"

"Not at all. I'll book us a flight."

"No thanks, Arthur. I need to stop by EuroEnterprises for some business, and I'll take the company jet back."

He hesitated for a moment, his face hopeful, as if he were certain she would ask him to join her. She remained quiet, and Holt finally understood today was not a social climbing day.

Outside the door to John Stone's office, Mai hesitated then tapped a tattoo on the door, a signal between them. She opened it and stepped inside, closing the door behind her. John stood at the window that overlooked the Thames, hands in his pockets, his head bent.

"Everything all right?" she asked.

He turned to look at her, forcing a smile. "Yes, one of those things. Agents miss a report-in time."

"Does that happen often?" He shrugged. "Can I know who they are?"

"Bukharin and Nelson. I'm not worried. They're good agents. Good work with Fintan Maitland." He pointed to one of the Queen Anne chairs. She sat in one, and he sat down in its twin, at an angle to her.

"That's what I wanted to talk about," she said.

"I read your report. No need to debrief."

"I wanted to talk about it last night, but you didn't come home."

"I'm sorry, my dear," he said, and he was earnest. "I love nothing more than coming home to you, especially after we haven't seen each other in a while, but the overdue agents had my attention."

"You look tired. When was the last time you ate?"

"Now, don't be a mother hen. I'm fine. What did you want to talk about?"

"What I did to Fintan doesn't feel right."

"He has been passing money to the IRA. That is a fact."

"I believe that, but did we have to answer his wrong with another wrong?"

"What you did wasn't wrong."

"That's debatable. I used a family connection to blackmail someone into doing something, and now his life is in danger."

Stone sighed and rubbed his unshaven face. "Look, darling, espionage is never black and white. We are always in the shades of gray. Sometimes we do distasteful things to keep something far more distasteful from happening. Sometimes we choose the lesser wrong for the greater good. I know that sounds like a pep talk, but it's the truth. We have to lie, cheat, and steal at times to achieve our ends, and, yes, it often leaves a bad taste in one's mouth. But it has to be done. I know that. Your parents knew that. Oh, yes, we often had qualms, but the bigger picture always overcomes them."

"I'll try to think of the 'bigger picture' when someone tells me Fintan's body was found tarred, feathered, and hanging from a lamp post."

"Darling, it's all right to have qualms, but you understand if you pursue this endeavor you will occasionally have to put them aside?"

"Yes, I understand that on a certain level. My mother and father had to make these decisions, right?"

"Of course, but they—and I—had the war as impetus for the gray areas. In some ways that's easier. The Cold War offers more grays in more shades, but I never led you to believe that this was easy."

"No, you didn't, and I do understand the import of what The Directorate does."

"But?"

"No but. Some concepts take getting used to."

"I know, and you've got time to do that. Are you up for something less troubling than recruiting?"

"Yes, of course."

"I think you need to get back into riding, eventing, cross-country."

"I have missed riding."

"I thought all those airplanes would have made you forget about four-legged transportation."

She smiled for the first time since her last conversation with Fintan. "Whom shall I spy on?"

- 4 -

ANOTHER BRICK IN THE WALL

Northern Virginia, 1979

Alexei had dozed on the short elevator ride to the penthouse condo. The doors chimed when the car reached his floor, and he had opened one eye to find the offending alarm only to see he was home. He was quiet and deft with the key in the lock and opened the door to find the chandelier over the dining table dimmed and Roisin O'Saidh seated there, a glass of whiskey at hand and a folder of papers before her.

Who, he wondered, drank whiskey at two-thirty in the morning? The Irish apparently.

O'Saidh must have conceded that it was the middle of the night by not putting her dark chestnut hair in its habitual bun, but she had made up her eyes and donned a business suit. Alexei glanced around and saw no sign that Mai was awake. He dropped his bag by the door and walked across the open space of the condo to the dining area. O'Saidh lifted her glass to drink and studied him over the rim with eyes that were as dead as his own.

"What are you doing up?" he asked her. His eyes went to the folder, emblazoned with a bow and arrow, the logo of EuroEnterprises, Mai's business consortium, of which O'Saidh was the Chief Operating Officer.

"I intercepted the call from your concierge downstairs. He told me you were on your way here from the airport."

"Why didn't Mai answer the call?"

"Because she's asleep, and I didn't want her disturbed."

"How is she?" Alexei asked.

"Nice of you to ask," O'Saidh said.

Alexei's jet lag almost made him take the bait. "How is she?"

21

"Better. Still weak. Still sleeps most of the day, but she's alive. That's all that matters. How was the important business that took you away? Blonde or brunette?"

His hands almost fisted, but he caught himself. "I'm sorry to have interrupted your work, Roisin," he said. "I'll be getting to bed."

"Not in her bed."

"It's our bed, and if she doesn't want me in it, she'll tell me."

O'Saidh lay a hand on the file folder. "I have something here I'd like you to review," she said.

His frown deepened. Mai's business concerns were something he stayed away from because, despite what the law might say about what he was entitled to, he wanted no interest in them. "What is it?"

O'Saidh narrowed her hazel eyes at him and smiled, a predatory expression he noted. "A divorce settlement. It's extremely generous."

Alexei shook his head, as if the fatigue had blocked his hearing, and worked to keep his anger under control. "Did Mai request that?"

"As I said, it's generous, but I'm willing to negotiate. The top limit is twenty-five million. I can make the pen-and-ink change right now, if you'll sign the papers."

"Did Mai request this?" he asked again, already tired of having to repeat himself.

"I do nothing except in her interests."

"You manage her business interests, not her personal life."

"They're interchangeable, me bucko. She can do better than you."

"And how would you know? Your deepest relationship is with an accounts receivable ledger. If divorce is to be discussed, that will be between Mai and me."

"Mai and you? When was there ever a Mai and you? Have you been here? No, I'm the one who's had to dose her with painkillers for the past three days when you decided to up and leave after she took five Loyalist bullets."

"I know. I was there."

"No, you weren't, not when it happened. You weren't there, and she almost died, you bastard. I want you gone. I'll make it twenty-eight million."

"Does she know how fast and loose you play with her money, Roisin? Good night." He turned and walked away.

"Don't turn your back on me," O'Saidh called to him, but he ignored her.

When he turned the knob on the bedroom door, he found it locked. He clenched the knob tighter to keep him from clenching the Irishwoman's throat with the same intensity. With the image of that in mind, he went to the kitchen and rummaged through a drawer, then another, not finding what he wanted.

"Where's the fucking key?" he asked the woman.

O'Saidh leaned back in the dining chair and sipped whiskey. "I tossed it off the balcony. Good luck finding it this time of night."

"Are you fucking kidding me? What's the point of this?"

"Another brick in the wall I'm building between you and her. That's all, me bucko. Thirty million."

His eyes drifted to his right, to the expensive chef's knives in their block on the counter, and his hand actually twitched in their direction before he caught himself.

When he looked at her, he saw she wasn't phased by the thousand-mile stare he gave her. Any other time, that he hadn't intimidated her would have impressed him. "No need to count out the money, Roisin," he said. "I'm not married to her for that."

"Every man has a price, Bukharin. I'll find yours."

Alexei took out his wallet and removed a credit card and went back to the door. He slipped the lock easily and looked over his shoulder before he turned the knob.

"Next time, install a dead bolt," he said and went inside the bedroom, shutting and locking the door behind him.

There was enough moon through the skylights he could see Mai in bed, curled up on her right side, a position she'd found in the hospital in Belfast where she was in the least pain. His feet were silent as he went to the bedside table and checked the medication log. Roisin O'Saidh might be able to piss him off in a half-minute, but she'd been fastidious about making sure Mai got her pain medications and antibiotics on time.

He reached out and lay his hand on her forehead. Cool. He let his hand linger for a moment before he crept through the dark to the bathroom. He could make his way around this place blindfolded, so there was no need to disturb her sleep with a light. When he came back out, he tossed his suit and shirt across a chair then went to the empty side of the bed and slipped beneath the covers. He was glad he'd left his singlet and boxers on as he slid next to her and inhaled the scent of her hair. Even then, he still had to force his body not to react to her sexually. Merely, he was glad to be this close to her, to feel the fact that she breathed on her own.

The memory of breathing for her as she bled her life out was too fresh, a near-miss that had been too near, and he wouldn't let it intrude. He rested a hand on her hip and placed a chaste kiss on her shoulder.

"I'm awake," she murmured.

"Sorry."

"Well, Roisin's 'Don't turn your back on me' was pretty loud."

"You heard?"

"Just the end. I didn't know she locked the bloody door. Help me turn over," she said.

"No, I'll switch sides."

The king-sized bed had always felt like a gulf to him, though it had its uses for one of their no-holds-barred interludes of sex. As it was, he was able to shift so that he faced her without her having to disturb her comfortable position. He watched her eyes wander his face, and he got as close as he could without her feeling that he wanted her.

"How did the mission go?" she asked.

"A minor SS functionary. With dementia. He wasn't worth the trip. It was Nigel Hume's way of showing me I don't get to dictate my actions. I didn't want to leave. You know that."

He thought she nodded but wasn't certain.

"What was the deal with Roisin?" she asked.

"She blames me, which is not far from the truth that I blame myself for what happened."

"Actually, I blame the Loyalist bastard with the gun," Mai said. "I've had enough time to understand you had to go get the person who was kidnapped. She was an innocent."

"Mai, I didn't choose…"

"I said I understand."

Their eyes locked, and all he wanted to do was fall asleep with the image of her eyes in mind. He'd almost lost her, and that had brought emotions close to the surface, emotions that were too dangerous.

"Roisin is sitting in the dining room with whiskey and divorce papers," he said.

He felt her body stiffen, saw her purse her lips with the pain that caused. "Is that what you want?" she asked, her voice flat.

"I was going to ask you the same thing."

"I didn't tell her to do that."

"She offered me thirty million to sign."

"Of my money?"

"Well, it's not hers."

"Tempted?"

"Not in the least."

Her body relaxed, and she managed to shift closer to him. They kissed, for a while, too long for his comfort. Mai laughed softly when he edged his lower body away from her. "Sorry," she said. "I'm not quite feeling up to it. I wish I were."

His hand was tight on her hip. "I wish you were, too."

"Well, yes, for that reason, as well."

"As well?"

"It's too bad we can't be noisy about it and fluster the Virgin Queen in there."

"The what?"

"That's what her staff call her. She probably knows it, but it's more fun thinking that she doesn't."

"You don't seriously think she is, do you?"

"A virgin? No. She doesn't know that I know, but she uses a small, discrete French escort service."

"You spy on your own business manager?"

"Of course. How else do I keep her honest?"

"An escort service? For men, I assume."

"Yes. Younger than she, no less."

He glanced toward the door. "Well, I hope I won't look too smug over coffee in the morning."

"Don't you dare tease her about it. Leave that to me for the right occasion."

"Trying to talk your husband into a divorce isn't the right occasion?"

"Yes, well, I'll have to have the mind-your-own-business discussion again." She gave a sigh. "I'm glad you're home."

His hand moved from her hip to her cup her cheek. "I'm glad you're here," he murmured.

He saw the tears pool in her eyes, and she blinked them away. Her face transformed, hardening into an expression he'd never seen on her before.

"One time, Alexei," she said. "That's all you get to go rescue former lovers while I get shot to pieces. Understand?"

"Understood."

Roisin O'Saidh slept on her back, her hair in a single braid that lay across her pillow. In an hour or so, it would be dawn, and, come hell or high water, this would be done.

The swiftness had the intended effect. A hand over the mouth, a high-powered flashlight in the eyes brought the Irishwoman awake.

"See how easy it could be done?" came the question. "If I had a knife, you'd be dead before you could wake up."

O'Saidh's eyes widened, and she looked away from the light, tears running into her hair.

"We each have a place in life. I know what mine is, and this is a reminder what yours is. Understand me? Nod, if you do." The woman's head bobbed, rustling against the pillow. "It's time for you to do what it is you were hired to do. First thing in the morning. No need to say a word about why. Pack and go. Nod again."

O'Saidh obeyed, more tears falling, their trails shining in the flashlight's beam.

The light switched off, the hand was removed, and a weight left the side of the bed.

"Why?" O'Saidh asked, her voice a croak.

In the dark, Mai Fisher turned back to the woman she was closer to than she had been to her own, long-dead mother. She had to brace a hand on the door jamb to stay upright.

"You wanted a choice to be made," Mai said. "I've done the choosing. Have a good flight home, Roisin."

- 5 -

A LITTLE ROMANCE

Paris, 1981

"Hold my hand and walk," Alexei said.

"You aren't usually so romantic," Mai replied as she slipped her hand in his. His hand adjusted, so their fingers intertwined.

"I can be very romantic," he said, "as you well know. I think we'd be less suspicious following our quarry if we looked like a couple in love in the City of Lights."

Yes, she thought, appearances are everything. And nothing.

"Here we are," she murmured, "thespians of espionage."

She heard Alexei's low chuckle and felt his fingers squeeze hers.

"There," he said, "he's headed to the street market. I'll be the shopper. You keep an eye on him."

The market did a brisk business, from chefs buying for the dinner fare to housewives buying for their families. Given Paris' place in the long history of espionage, Mai thought it likely she and Alexei were not the first spies here. And Alexei, the gourmet cook, blended, though he drew amused laughter at his bad French.

She suspected she was the alien, the outsider; she couldn't tell a ripe avocado from a stone, but Alexei played his part well, holding up fruits and vegetables for her approval.

He paid for a bright, red apple, took out his pocket knife, and began to pare off slices for them both as they walked, keeping the man in view.

The stiff, vinyl coat the man wore reminded her of some beetle's carapace. It didn't flow when he walked; it rode on him like a suit of armor. A disguise, she supposed, for anyone who might recognize him.

Among the man's purchases from the market were a loaf of bread, some expensive chocolates, a bottle of red wine—all tucked away in a plain, canvas carryall—and an armful of yellow roses.

"He's a cliché," Alexei said.

"But yellow roses mean 'I care,' and because you've never brought me flowers, don't assume he's a cliché," Mai replied.

Alexei looked at her, a frown creasing his broad forehead.

"No, you've never brought me flowers."

"You detest shallow gestures," he said.

"That's true, but…"

"I'll bring you flowers."

"It should be spontaneous."

"It'll be a surprise."

The continued consumption of the apple and the whispered conversation covered them well. Their quarry never noticed when they turned down the same street as he. Alexei slowed their pace and tossed the apple core into a trash bin as they passed. The man's steps, however, quickened, and before he could ascend the stairs to a house at the end of a row, the door flew open. A young woman, chic in a knee-length black skirt and a white silk blouse, bounded down the stairs and into the man's arms, her mouth pressing against his. Handling the carryall, the flowers, and his lover was a bit much for him, but he broke the kiss to glance over his shoulder.

Deftly, Alexei turned Mai toward one of the houses and pointed at something about the architecture. When Mai looked around again the man and woman climbed the steps arm in arm. The door closed behind them.

Mindful the man might watch the street from a window of the house, Alexei and Mai continued their stroll until they rounded a corner. Now out of sight of the house, they jogged down an alley to the rowhouse directly across from the other. From his pocket, Alexei took a key, let them in, and led the way up the stairs to the third floor.

In a small bedroom, surveillance equipment sat ready for them—a parabolic mic, a tape recorder, a video camera, and an SLR with a zoom lens. Alexei went for the parabolic mic, taking it up as he put on the headset. He turned on the recorder. Mai made certain the video camera lined up with the top-floor bedroom of the other house. She checked the SLR and the camera bag and saw she had plenty of film.

"She's effusing over the flowers," Alexei said, listening. "A little too much, maybe."

"She knows what she's doing," Mai replied.

It was the oldest of gambits: pick a politician you wanted to influence, discover his weakness—in this case women a third his age—use someone to seduce him, take pictures of their liaisons, and use those to get him to do what you wanted. Aptly called a honey trap, it was a tried and true device.

"Ah, they're headed to the bedroom," Alexei said. "Stand-by on the camera."

"I hope she can convince him to leave the curtains open this time," Mai said. "But I know how much you enjoy being a voyeur." She heard his low chuckle at her mock disapproval.

Mai stood back, far enough from the window so no one from the street or the house across the way could see her and the camera. In the corner of her eye, she saw Alexei adjust the angle of the mic as well. She snapped a few shots of their honey trap moving about the room, her lover staying in the shadows. The woman had her back to the window, but Mai saw her hands, moving as she talked; then, the woman turned, looked directly at Mai's window, and pushed the curtains further open. Mai saw the woman's amused smile.

The stage was set. The ornate queen-sized bed was in perfect alignment with the cameras, and the woman urged the man to sit on the end of the bed. Her hands worked on opening his trousers, and Mai detached as she snapped away—close-ups of the man's face as he watched the woman give him head, his fist clenched in her hair.

Within a few minutes they were both naked and on the bed, and Mai had to admit for a man in his sixties, their subject was holding his own. She glanced to her left. Alexei had his eye glued to the viewfinder on the video-camera. She shook her head and resumed taking pictures.

"Well," she said, "I have lovely pictures of his ass. She needs to flip him." Again, she heard Alexei's throaty chuckle. "All my training and preparation, and why do I feel like some sleazy private detective?"

"I prefer to think of it as tradecraft. That signatory government needs his vote at the Security Council. This is the best way of any to assure he votes the right way."

"And you have no qualms at all," she stated.

"It gets the job done. And there. You have your flip."

Mai worked the lens to capture not only the man's face but the woman's body moving up and down. She thought perhaps she should give them some privacy, but she continued to take pictures, including the post-coital shots of the couple snuggling naked atop the bedcovers. That lasted only a few minutes, and, after an exchange of kisses, the two got up from the bed. Mai took pictures of the man getting dressed. The woman, however, donned only a dark blue, satin bathrobe. The two of them left the bedroom.

Alexei put on the headphones again. "She's thanking him for the flowers and wine," he said. "She's asking when she'll see him again, and he's told her in two days."

"We have enough, surely?" Mai asked, not particularly wanting to do this again.

She brought the camera back up to her eye as the front door of the house opened. She took a shot of the man and woman kissing on the doorstep, the robe falling open and his hand on her breast; she included several face-on shots in full daylight, as he turned and strode down the steps and back up the street. It was a face anyone in his country would recognize.

The woman looked from the doorway to the windows Mai and Alexei were behind. Mai stepped closer to her window and gave a thumbs-up. The woman nodded, smiled, and disappeared behind the closed door.

In two days when the man came for his next assignation, he would find an empty house with a "For Let" sign on the front door.

Mai and Alexei packed up the equipment and left it for the courier who would pick it up later. The tape recording, video cassette, and film went into Mai's bag. After Alexei used the bathroom, they exited through the rear of the house again but didn't retrace their steps. They strolled in a different direction, to assure they didn't run into the famous statesman they were about to blackmail.

When Alexei opened the door to their suite at the Paris Hilton, he turned to her and smiled before he stepped aside. In the center of the foyer table sat a crystal vase holding two dozen, red roses.

"Surprised?" he asked.

"How did you…"

"The side trip to the bathroom covered my call to the concierge. Well, are you surprised?"

"Yes, I suppose I am."

He leaned over, kissed her cheek, and whispered to her how she could thank him. Mai laughed and took his hand, leading him toward the bedroom. "Why did you pick red?" she asked him.

"I grew up in Russia, *dushenka*. Red is my favorite color," he said, with a smile.

That would be the only reason, she knew. Alexei wouldn't know red roses meant love. If he had, they wouldn't have been red.

- 6 -

HONOR

New York, 1981

The U.N. Ambassador didn't listen to the banter from his companions in the elevator, most of it in languages he didn't know. He kept his sunglasses on, however, so he could study the backsides of the women in the elevator. Tucked back in a corner, the Ambassador wondered if the U.N. picked the secretarial staff from the same fashion model mold. Not that he was complaining. No, he considered it a perk of office.

When the doors opened on his floor, he was polite in excusing himself but managed to brush against at least two of the women on his exit. On the stroll to his office, he nodded to acquaintances, got side-tracked by other ambassadors, but arrived at his office on time.

A new girl was at the administrative assistant's desk, and his practiced eye gave her a once-over. An unsmiling face, reddish hair in a tight French braid, no-nonsense black business suit. Skirt just above the knee he noticed when she stood, and her legs—what he could see—and her figure were nice, very nice. In her twenties, he guessed, very luminous dark yes, modest yet effective make-up. He compared her with his usual assistant and decided today would be a good day, indeed.

"*Bon jour, monsieur ambassadeur,*" she said, her French excellent.

"Well, good morning," he said in his equally good English. "Where's Vivien?"

"Called away for a family emergency," the girl said. "I'm from the pool."

"Ah, English I hear."

"Yes, sir."

"And how long will Vivien be away?"

31

"The pool administrator didn't say, Mr. Ambassador."

"Well, I'm sure we'll make the best of it," he said, with a smile.

He allowed her to see his appreciation, and her eyes dipped demurely to the floor. Ah, reluctance. That made it so much more challenging, but he'd found his money, his position here and at home, and the fact that he had aged well made him very attractive to young women.

"Give me a half-hour to make some phone calls and bring today's mail in," he told her. "We'll go over it together and compose the replies, yes?"

"Of course, sir," she said. She remained standing until he went into his office.

At his desk, where the girl had arranged his phone messages, he sat and flipped through them, seeking one name in particular. He sat back with a sigh when he didn't see it and pondered why Annette wasn't returning his calls. Perhaps she was upset at the message he'd left for her explaining that he had to postpone their upcoming rendezvous. How sweet that she would pine for him.

After a moment he rose and walked to the window, where he stood, hands clasped behind him. Tour boats went by on their way up the East River. Traffic on the Queensboro Bridge was still bumper to bumper, and the tiny U Thant Island seemed like a smear of sludge on the brownish blue water.

He was being somewhat indiscrete with his continued attempts to contact Annette. She certainly wasn't his only mistress, but she was the most enlivening in a while. He thought back over their last encounter at her flat in Paris, and that brought a smile to his face. Annette was not only very athletic, but she loved to give him oral sex. The French were much more advanced in this area than the women of his country. Of course, his country was a theocracy with a religion that insisted women were of better use in the home, so there was no reason why his countrywomen should have knowledge of exotic sexual practices, but still... A man got tired of fucking wives who didn't want to uncover themselves or who saw it as an unpleasant duty instead of an opportunity for being adventuresome. Neither of his wives would even sleep through the night with him, and he often woke to an empty bed.

Not with Annette. On the rare occasions when he could spend the entire night, he enjoyed waking first and watching her sleep, especially when she had discarded the bedcovers in the night and he could appreciate her incredible body.

Now, the new girl at the desk. Her body was younger than Annette's by at least a decade. That would be an interesting view.

When the knock came on the door, he realized how lost in his salacious thoughts he'd been. He fixed a charming smile on his face and called out, "Come in."

The girl entered, bearing a modest stack of mail, and he saw she wore dark red, high-heel shoes. What was it the American women called them? Ah, yes. Fuck-me pumps. He smiled and wondered if he could persuade her to keep them on in bed.

"Ah," he said, "here we are. Please sit down."

She waited until he sat down behind his desk to perch on the edge of the chair across from him. When he smiled at her again, her face stayed immobile. Well, some of them liked to put up a business-like front.

He watched as she took a large, sealed envelope from the stack of mail she carried. The rest, she set aside.

"I think you should open this first," she said.

"My dear, isn't that your job?" he said, teasing.

"When you open it you'll see why I didn't."

Now, this was intriguing. Was this perhaps some little game she played? Well, the door to the office did lock.

He had no letter opener and had to find his scissors in the desk drawer to cut open the envelope, and he spilled the contents onto his desk. Photographs, it seemed, a dozen or more. He turned them over to view the top one and felt his heart lurch.

The Ambassador dropped the photos as if they'd burned his hands. He pushed his chair away from the table, and Mai Fisher was fascinated by the abrupt appearance of sweat on his face—a slick more than a sheen.

Mai stood, picked up the stack of photographs, and placed them one-by-one on the desktop, arranged so the Ambassador could see them. When she looked at him again, she saw that he wept.

"These are your copies," she said. "I have the originals and the negatives, and if I don't return to my office by the close of business today, copies will go to *The Sun*. Your king could see them by tomorrow. He's a long-time subscriber."

"Wh..who are you?"

"That's irrelevant. Do I have your attention?"

He jerked to his feet and stepped toward her, stopped by the large desk between them. His face contorted to the point where he wouldn't be recognized as the handsome, older man in the photographs.

"I demand to know who you are!" he shouted.

"Sit down," she said.

His hands, fingers bent and clutching at air, came up. "I will kill you, you bitch, you whore. I will…"

Mai drew her gun and leveled it at his head. "I said sit down."

The hands clenched into fists, but he sat, or rather, slumped in his chair, his glare hostile.

"That's better," Mai said. She holstered her gun and re-seated herself.

"What is the price for all the copies of this, this garbage?" he asked, one hand flicking toward the arrayed photos.

"It's a simple price, really, but there'll be no exchange of goods."

"I will not cooperate until I can be assured I will get the originals, the negatives, and all copies."

Mai gave him a hint of a smile. "I'm going out on a limb here and assume you don't want your government or your family to see these pictures. Adultery in your country is punishable by death, or is that only women who are executed for it?"

"Whore!"

"No, that was the woman in the photos."

She saw him pale, so much so she thought he might faint, but he shook his head, took out a handkerchief, and mopped his forehead and eyes.

"She is no whore," the Ambassador said.

"I beg to differ. She did exactly what we paid her to do."

"Who do you work for?"

Mai smiled and relaxed in the chair. "That's need to know, Mr. Ambassador."

"What did you do to Annette to make her do this?" he demanded.

"Oh, she was happy to volunteer. You thought she was French, but you'd be half right. Her father was French, but her mother was from your country. You knew her mother quite well. She was your half-sister, whom you and your brothers murdered thirty years ago in France."

"No!"

"Yes. Annette's father made certain she understood her mother had been the victim of an honor killing and who had been responsible."

"Impossible. My sister didn't have a child."

"She did. She and her husband managed to hide that because they were afraid your family would drag her back to your homeland and force her to marry when she was twelve, like your sister."

"My sister was an adulterer. She deserved to die."

"You, sir, are an adulterer as well, and the Quran forbids incest. Annette is your niece, after all."

"How dare you speak of the Holy Quran! You have no understanding of my religion…"

"No, I don't, and I'm glad. Anyway, Annette agreed to do this for justice."

"Justice? Justice? I'm the one who has been done an injustice. Lied to and blackmailed by whores."

"Annette wanted justice for her mother, whom you murdered when she was three, you bastard."

The Ambassador raised his hand and waved it again, to dismiss her. "You drone at me, little bee," he said. "Your words are nothing but incomprehensible buzzing."

"That may be the case, but you have a choice to make. Utter humiliation at home or do what I say. Now, I understand your king really has no moral issues about how many women you fuck. He's got quite the unofficial harem himself, but he really doesn't like it when his government officials' actions don't harmonize with the image of piety he's established for your country. I don't imagine he'll be too happy to see pictures of your face—or your ass—for the world to see. And the accompanying copy will tell the whole sordid story of your niece Annette and her mother, your sister, whom your family has denied to the world."

The Ambassador slammed a fist on his desk. "As it should be!"

"Why? Because she dared to love someone you didn't pick for her?"

He pointed a finger at her. "You cannot understand."

"I understand better than you know, Mr. Ambassador. Now, if you don't want those pictures made public, start listening to me."

The Ambassador wiped his face again and flicked his fingers at her to continue.

"There is a resolution before the General Assembly this afternoon, for which you have gone on record stating you will vote no. Change your vote to yes."

His eyebrows lifted. "That is all?"

"For now. There may be other votes in future. That's why I hold onto the negatives."

His eyes narrowing, he leaned forward, studying her. "Are you Mossad?"

Mai laughed and shook her head. "I'm not the agent of any government. Do you understand what you have to do? Have I explained myself clearly?"

"Yes."

"I'll be in the gallery this afternoon, watching the session. If you vote no, all it takes is one phone call, and those photos appear tomorrow in *The Sun*."

"You're not the only person who can blackmail," the Ambassador said, smiling at her.

"Oh, I've already blackmailed *The Sun*'s publisher. The photos will be published if I request it. Are we clear?" The smirk left his face.

He considered it far longer than she was comfortable with, but he gave her a single, curt nod. "I will vote yes."

Mai stood and smoothed her skirt. "I'm afraid you'll be without an admin for today. Vivien will be back tomorrow," she said and turned to go.

"Wait. Take those filthy pictures with you."

"Please, keep them as souvenirs. Better yet, as a reminder that I may have other requests."

Mai was at the door when she heard the ambassador ask, "How do you sleep at night?"

She turned back and gave him her dazzling smile. "Far better than you will from now on, I suspect. Don't forget the session this afternoon. Remember, I'll be watching. Good day."

- 7 -

INCONSEQUENTIAL PROMISES

West Suffolk, England, 1982

Maintaining a cover meant she slept in a guest room of the massive house, and Alexei bunked in the servant's quarters. In this day and age, it was such an anachronism to separate the classes, but some gentry couldn't let go of the things that set them apart.

Well, that, and it would be too difficult to explain why her "chauffeur" was staying in her room, though she found herself somewhat eager in awaiting his knock on the door of the manor's library. Not for a tryst, though perhaps she could talk him into it later, after dispensing with this little mission.

Not every member of British aristocracy had the funds to support the image and station they wanted to put on display. That was obvious from this house, in the earl's family for nearly 300 years. Limited income meant that all the resources went to making the outside presentable, but the decay was beginning to show on the inside.

One whole wing of the house was closed off—for "renovation," the earl had explained. Even during the day, curtains were drawn and lighting kept low so no one could see the fading upholstery and the frayed drapery or that the silver service at dinner wasn't really silver. A good match overall, down to the family crest, but silver plate all the same.

The earl had gone to Eton with her father, Mai remembered, and she'd encountered the son at the various events and country parties she'd attended before going to America to become a spy. She had no qualms about spying on an acquaintance, given what he was doing to keep up appearances.

The earl wasn't the perpetrator. That was his son, who worked in the Home Office and had access to information the Soviet Union paid a great deal to obtain. There was, however, collusion between father and son: Son obtained the secrets; Father passed them along under the guise of trade and agricultural products negotiations. Regardless, the earl and his son had dug themselves a pretty big hole of treason. Without proof it was simply a rumor.

She checked her watch. Alexei was two minutes late. He was rarely late for anything.

Although she'd already determined there were no listening devices or hidden video cameras, except for the ones she'd placed here, she did a sweep of the circular room again, noting the old, first editions were missing—probably sold off—and the marble and granite inlaid compass rose that was the centerpiece of the library's floor had pieces missing from it. The décor was an odd mixture of the old world—family portraits, hunting scenes, and Tudor-era artifacts—and the modern: an apple done in lead crystal and the size of a melon, resting on a marble and brass pedestal that probably once displayed a Ming vase.

On the hearth was a massive soapstone footrest carved in the shape of a beetle, a scarab such as no pharaoh had ever beheld. It was squat and ugly and suggested to her people trying to keep up the image of being art collectors.

She checked her watch again. Five minutes late. Damn. She hoped neither the earl nor his son woke and decided a good book would get him back to sleep. She walked to the French doors that led onto the terrace. Beyond that was a Japanese garden, not an English one, a feature added by one of the earl's ancestors in the 1800's. A stream had been re-directed to wind its way through the garden and beneath a bridge, which had been dismantled in Kyoto and reassembled here. The earl's family was the only one at the time to have an actual Japanese gardener, and that corner of the garden with the bridge and the willows and the koi pond had been immortalized in a painting by the current Prince of Wales.

Another reason why getting solid proof was important. His Royal Highness would certainly come to the defense of an old friend, the earl, unless he could be shown irrefutable evidence. Hence, a certain set of documents crossed the son's desk at Home Office, information that, on the surface, would be of obvious interest to his Soviet masters. If a copy of the papers was in the earl's safe, it could only be traced back to his son. The mission wasn't to take the papers but rather photograph them in situ. Later, they'd follow the earl to photograph him passing them on to whom he thought was a Soviet agent.

This time Mai sighed when she checked her watch. Ten minutes late. She heard the soft tap on the door, one knock followed a beat later by three quick ones. She crossed to the door and opened it just enough for Alexei to enter. She closed it and locked it again from the inside.

The moonlight was enough to show her his flushed face, unfastened cuffs, and a shirt tucked in his pants without much care. He noticed her scrutiny and stepped closer to place a kiss on her neck. She smelled his familiar scent and something more. Cheap perfume and sex. She eased away from his touch.

"I got the key," he whispered, "and made a copy."

I bet you did, she thought. "From the downstairs maid or the upstairs one?" she asked.

He showed her no chagrin. He never did. Where she would have broken into the son's bedroom to locate the key, Alexei did it by seducing a member of the household. It was no matter, except that it really was.

"The original is safely back where it came from," was all he said.

"Let's get moving," Mai said. "I feeling like a sitting duck here."

They walked to the family portrait of the first earl, and Alexei used a small penlight taken from his pocket to examine the frame for wires or connections to an alarm system. Finding nothing, he lifted the frame off the wall and set it aside.

A fairly modern safe had been recessed into the wall with a keypad lock, not a combination one.

"Well, hell," Alexei muttered.

"So, the maid didn't know the combination?" Mai asked, her sarcasm still sharp.

"Say something useful, Mai," Alexei said, a snap at her. Even in the scant light, she saw his narrowed eyes.

"The hidden camera showed the strongbox and the key, not the safe. Sorry. I had to put the camera where it wouldn't be seen."

"I didn't ask you to apologize, and I wasn't criticizing. I was getting you back on topic."

As was often the case, she suppressed the surge of anger and walked to the earl's desk where she began to rifle the contents of the drawers. After a moment, he was at her side, joining her in the search.

In the bottom right drawer, in a hanging folder labeled "Household," Mai found the safe's owner's manual. She held it up for Alexei to see.

"It won't be that simple, Mai," he said, his tone approaching condescension.

Mai thumbed through the booklet and found the page with the directions for setting the combination. A box at the bottom of the page was labeled, "Enter your combination here." She smiled and showed the four numbers to Alexei.

"Or that's a plant, and I enter those four numbers, and an alarm goes off," he said.

"Well, blowing it up is a bit noisy and defeats the purpose," she replied.

"There's no reason for you to be testy," he said. "We're on a mission." He glanced again at the numbers, took a pencil from the desk, then returned to the safe while Mai replaced the booklet in the folder exactly where she'd found it.

At his side again, she watched him punch the numbers in with the eraser end of the pencil. He slipped his hand up inside his sleeve so he'd leave no fingerprints on the safe's handle. He was deliberate in opening the safe, and they both waited a moment, listening for the sound of running footsteps. When nothing seemed forthcoming, Alexei eased the door open and used the penlight again to check for trip wires or electronic beams across the safe's opening.

When he was satisfied there were no booby-traps or alarm trips, again he covered his hands with his shirtsleeves and drew the small strongbox from the safe. That he placed on a table nearby and took the key from his pocket. The miniature padlock on the box opened without a problem, but Alexei moved to one side before he opened the box itself in case it was the item booby-trapped. Mai understood the caution, but her impatience flared. She wanted to be out of this library before they got caught.

Nothing went "bang" nor did acid destroy the contents, and Alexei took a nondescript file folder from the box and opened it. Mai had to stand close to him to verify the papers were copies of the planted ones, and the reek of perfume and sex assailed her again. Of course, if he'd gone to shower first, that would have made him even later.

"These are the papers," Alexei said.

"Agreed, but I have my camera," she replied.

He spread them on the desk, and she used the miniature camera to take pictures of the papers, the strongbox, the safe, and the library. Alexei replaced the file folder with papers in the box and returned it to the safe. The picture back in place, they were done.

Mai again took note of the time. "We shouldn't leave through the door to the house," she said.

"Why not?"

"I know how a house this size works," she whispered. "It's time for the cooks and the maids to be up, at least all the maids except one. We should go out through the terrace doors and into the garden so no one in the kitchen and the backstairs will see us."

She watched his mouth tighten into a thin line, but he said, "All right, I'll go first. Wait five and leave."

She nodded and waited until he was almost at the door. "What did you promise her?" she asked.

He turned to her and almost pulled off the lie. "Who?"

"The maid. What did you promise her in exchange for the key, the nicking of which could cost her a job?"

"Nothing of consequence."

"Do you like that they pine after you?" she asked. "All the women you use. Does it appeal to your ego?"

"Can we have this conversation some other time and place?"

"Let's make an appointment, shall we?"

He took a few steps back toward her. "You and I, we're partners. For me, that's an unbreakable bond. You know that. What I do to achieve a mission doesn't affect that relationship. Now, I'm going back to my chauffeur's quarters…"

"Are you?"

"Yes." He turned from her and strode across the library, checked the area before he opened the French doors. He went outside and soon disappeared into the dark.

Mentally, she kicked herself. She should have kept her mouth shut. There was going to be a further lecture about the appropriate time and place to discuss personal matters. The truth was, they never had that honest of a conversation about Alexei's methods versus hers. By the time they got around to it, something had diffused her anger and disappointment. That something was her emotions, the one particular emotion she wasn't supposed to have for him. Her partner. If she'd accept that's all she was, his partner before his wife, she'd be the happier for it.

For a final time, her eyes took in all 360 degrees of the once-comely room before she, too, left through the French doors. She walked the garden, instead of going to her room, and stood, alone, on the bridge to watch the koi swim lazily in the moonlight..

- 8 -

A BEAUTIFUL DAY

Prague, Czechoslovakia, 1982

Mai Fisher made certain she turned the pages of her book at appropriate intervals to make it look as if she actually read it. Without moving her wrist, she checked her watch and saw her contact should be here any minute.

She lay the book down and picked up her coffee cup, her eyes glancing several tables away, where Alexei Bukharin sat, pretending to read a newspaper. His left hand moved and showed her two fingers. He'd spotted the contact on the approach.

She took another sip of coffee and made one more scan of the street, the sidewalks, and the outdoor café in this particular corner of Prague on a beautiful, late spring day. No hostiles that she could see. Alexei didn't see any either, or he would have given the abort signal. She picked up the book and feigned reading again.

The man with the pink, rosebud boutonnière in his right lapel weaved along the sidewalk as he constantly looked around. Mai winced at his calling too much attention to himself. When he stopped by her table and made it obvious he read the title of her book—to make certain she was his contact—she rose with a smile and took one of his hands in hers.

"Cousin Dusan," she said, not too soft, not too loud, "how good to see you. I'm so glad you could spare the time so we can catch up."

When they exchanged kisses on both cheeks, Mai felt his fear-sweat transfer to her lips. As they sat, she was circumspect about dabbing her mouth with her napkin. A waiter came over, and Dusan ordered an espresso. Mai watched his eyes dart about again and wondered how she could get him to stop standing out like a sore thumb. He took out a folded, white handkerchief and mopped his forehead and upper lip. His fingers smoothed his dark mustache, and she wondered if that were a signal to someone. Alexei had seen it, too. She saw him put down his paper and drink from his own cup as he now scanned the area.

Dusan started to speak, but Mai smiled and murmured, "Wait until the server comes and goes."

Dusan's espresso arrived, and he took up the small cup. It rattled against the saucer when he replaced it there after drinking.

"Relax, Dusan," Mai said, her voice soothing. "There's nothing to worry about."

"There's plenty to worry about," he said. "Ever since the lab accident, I've felt like I'm hanging over an abyss by my nails, and each day one more finger slips."

"Take a deep breath and tell me what happened," she said.

"It was a stupid thing, really," he said in his decent English. Mai was glad she didn't have to try using her scant Czech. "Two lab techs flirting where they shouldn't have been. I was working in the clean room with a contained atmosphere and in my protective suit; otherwise, I would have been…" He stopped, gulped more of his espresso, and the cup again rattled against the saucer.

"So, the lab techs were the ones who caused the accident?" Mai asked.

"What? Yes, yes. The male—a good young man, really, good at his job—reached for the young woman to give her a hug. She moved, he slipped, and crashed into the table holding the rack of Petri dishes. It fell to the floor, the dishes shattered, and… I'll never forget the look on their faces. They knew. The man was weeping and apologizing, and the woman walked calmly to the panic button and pressed it. Thank God, thank God, they had died before we had to burn the lab."

He sat back in his chair, pushing the coffee cup away from him. The handkerchief came out once more, and this time wiped tears from his cheeks.

"Was that the only lab in the facility working on this project?" Mai asked, still keeping her voice soft, to avoid being overheard and to calm Dusan.

"No, no. Those Petri dishes were in that lab for testing. The whole complex is involved in the project. If those two had suited up before…" He stopped, and the handkerchief wiped his eyes again.

"Dusan, I need for you to tell me what the Petri dishes held."

His nervous eyes twitched around the area again. "It is experimental, a combination of several virulent strains of anthrax," he murmured. "We are splicing the most deleterious effects of each into a new, super strain. We are determining if we can weaponize that new strain into an aerosol delivery system."

Her eyes shifted to Alexei, and he uncrossed his legs to show her he'd heard through the bug she wore. She looked back to Dusan. "Is all the research, the documentation, everything, confined to this one facility?"

"Yes, of course. It's very sensitive. When we brief our, uh, employers in the east, they come to us, and they take nothing away."

"No formulae, no processes?"

"No, no. The scientists do not come. Only the KGB and GRU."

Mai saw Alexei straighten from his slouch. Soviet military intelligence were involved, and she didn't need him to tell her how bad that could possibly be. "How close are you to perfecting the weaponization?" she asked Dusan.

Dusan looked down at his hands, which now wrung the handkerchief between them. "Two people died..." he began.

"From exposure to the strain, yes," she said, trying to suppress her impatience. "What about the weaponizing? How close?"

"Six, seven months, is what we say, but, realistically, at least a year."

Mai reached for her own coffee to lubricate her dry throat. When she was certain she wouldn't croak, she said, "Dusan, I need the location of the facility."

He shifted to the edge of his seat, as if he were about to stand and bolt. He shook his head several times. "I have already told you too much." More sweat broke out on his face, and he put the now-limp handkerchief to use once more.

"You contacted us."

"Yes, but I have a family, and I have said too much."

Mai's hand lay on his arm, appearing casual to anyone who might look, but she was squeezing the wrist, putting pressure on the joint there. "I need the location of the facility. Tell me, and we can get you and your family to safety."

His nervousness eased, and what might be hope filled his eyes. "You can do that?"

"Yes. Tell me."

He did more than that. He drew a map.

Alexei Bukharin was the first to reach the rendezvous point after placing his charges. He crouched in the woods, his eyes watching. In a few minutes he saw a slight figure moving from cover to cover and coming up the rise toward him. He lay his hand on the butt of his pistol until the figure was close enough he could recognize Mai.

She gave a low whistle, and he returned it. A moment later, she was at his side, catching her breath.

"Charges set?" he asked.

"Yes. The others are coming," she said.

He resumed his study of their immediate area. Four more figures moved from boulder to boulder or tree to tree. Once more, he wished an air strike had been feasible, but since this was a secret lab they'd learned of, they didn't even have the usual Soviet excuse to fall back on—fertilizer factory on the façade and chemical weapons production behind the scenes. No, a secret facility required a different approach.

From Dusan they had learned that only security staff were on the premises at night, so a daytime operation had been the only option. It did no good to blow up the research and the strains of anthrax only to have the same people start all over again somewhere else. Such an incursion as this was rare and dangerous, but daytime was the only way to assure all the personnel who could repeat the biological weapons research being conducted and supported by the Soviet Union would be on site.

Alexei had hand-picked his team. Mai was a given, of course, and the other four were top agents from The Directorate's offices around Europe. They'd spent a month watching the lab, its remoteness likely the reason the Warsaw Pact country didn't bother to put it in an urban area and disguise it.

Two of the team had gotten in on the cleaning detail, and between them they had an excellent plat of the building. They'd filmed and noted all the movements of personnel outside, found the weak points in the exterior security patrols, determined where the charges should go to ensure fire would destroy the entire complex, and developed the action plan, down to double-duty as snipers to pick off anyone trying to escape the burning facility.

Soon, the other four members of the team joined him and Mai, each reporting successful placement of their charges. From their supply cache hidden in a small cave, Alexei dispensed the four sniper rifles. Mai would be with him, as back up for the others. Sniping was against her principles, and he accepted that.

Because he was the team lead, it was up to him to send the signal to the electronic detonators placed in the Semtex. He waited until he heard each team member's radio report he or she was in place, and he murmured into his own radio, "Remember, we have twenty minutes before the military arrives, but everyone back off at fifteen. If you're not at the Vienna office in forty-eight hours, you'll have another twenty-four to get to the secondary site. After that, we'll assume you've been taken, and the appropriate protocols will commence. Respond to confirm you understand."

The responses came, clipped, cool, and he began his countdown. In his periphery, he saw Mai, alert, stoic, only the pulse racing at her throat showing her adrenaline was still up.

"...Three, two, one, Mark. Fifteen minutes," he finished and depressed the button on his transmitter.

The six explosions were close together, but he was able to confirm them all. The fuel tanks and gas lines blew at the same time, the concussion hard on the ears, and a ball of flame and smoke boiled skyward. A wash of heat swept over them. When the smoke billowed away, Alexei could see the building was fully engulfed.

He ventured another look at Mai. She was immobile, but she hadn't looked away. Her mission detachment was developing nicely, but the downturned line of her mouth told him she still had a conscience, and that was fine. For now. Until it interfered.

He tucked the transmitter away in his backpack, and together they watched. Only three people made it out, and their deaths were merciful—they had been human torches. Alexei touched her arm to indicate when it was time for them to leave.

As they picked their way to safety, Alexei decided it was best that Mai not learn until later that someone above their pay grade had decided Dusan's knowledge made him too much of a liability. He was at work today.

He put that out of mind and focused on the trek through the forest. It was, after all, a beautiful day.

- 9 -

RESOLVE

Eastern Europe, 1983

She dreamed of summers spent in Ireland with distant cousins in houses where the only place to dry your washing was on a line stretched across a narrow back yard. As a little girl, the clothes flapping in a breeze enthralled her, and, when she returned to the estate in England, she begged her governess to let her hang up her clothes that way.

The governess, Miss Rothschild, was all for making certain she wasn't spoiled and had already started the practice of having her wash out her own underwear at night, despite the fact her linen chest held dozens of sets. However, Miss Rothschild drew a figurative barrier at erecting a clothes-drying line next to some of the best gardens in Suffolk.

The dream left her calm when she woke to the sound of the padlock on the door rattling. Mai Fisher sat up from the mattress on the floor and shook weariness from her head. Her interrogator entered, his large frame blocking light from the doorway. He had a small table in one hand and a tray in the other. He set the table in the middle of her cell and placed the tray on it. He stepped back, arms pointing to the tray as if calling her attention to a present.

"Eat," he said. "Drink."

Her legs were still weak from the earlier session of water-boarding, weak because she'd strained so hard against the straps that lashed her to the board. Her stomach was too full of water to eat or drink, but if she didn't, he'd use it as an excuse for punishment.

As it was, she didn't rise fast enough for him. He clenched her shirt in one fist and hauled her to her feet. She stood on wobbly legs, and he hit her, backhanded. She had anticipated and turned her head, but his hand met her mouth hard enough to draw blood. The wall broke her fall, and she spat bloody phlegm onto the floor.

This time, his fist closed in her filthy hair, and he propelled her toward the table, his mouth at her ear. "Eat! Drink!" he shouted.

Ahead of her, the open door was an invitation. He would catch her, she knew, but that very act of escape might enrage him enough to kill her this time.

No. You were never dead until you were good and dead, and she wasn't there yet.

She picked up the good-sized hunk of black bread and managed a few bites, which she washed down with the strong tea. Some strength surged in her from that, and she took another bite of bread.

"You are at a crossroads," her interrogator said, walking to stand across the table from her. "You need to choose. Tell me what I want to know, and there will be reward. Persist in your stubbornness, and it will only end badly for you."

If the bruises covering most of her body were any testament, it was already pretty bad, and more than once she'd caught herself wondering if keeping her organization's secrets was worth what she'd undergone in the past two days.

"I thought we agreed," she said, as she chewed, "you've made some sort of mistake. You're asking me questions I don't know the answers to."

"You are a lying bitch," he said, face reddening, finger pointed at her. "I caught you, you little thief, with my ledger in your hands. You will tell me who you work for."

"I told you. I don't work for anyone. All right, I'm a thief. It takes money to keep up appearances, you know. So, I broke into your office looking for money, jewels, bonds, and all I came up with was a notebook with names of people I've never heard of. Useless to me. So, call the police, and accept my apology."

Though she hadn't been able to escape with the ledger, the names were fixed in her memory—people he dealt illegal arms to, illegal arms that killed innocent men, women, and children. Having the leverage to stop him was enough to keep her going.

He strode toward her, knocking the table over and sending the tray and the plate on it crashing to the floor. He slapped the remainder of the bread and the mug of tea from her hands. The fist he slammed into her stomach brought the scant food back up again, and she vomited on his boots.

His hand closed on her throat, and he forced her onto her back on the floor. He knelt on her thighs to keep her legs from being weapons, and she saw red as she tried to breathe. She watched as his other hand began to undo his belt and his pants. Panic threatened to overwhelm her as she waited for her conditioning to kick in and suppress it.

A magic wand would be great about now, she thought, as her hands searched along the floor for something, anything. Her vision was going gray now, but her fingers touched something and explored. Something tapered and sharp. A shard from the smashed plate.

Unmindful of cutting her fingers, she clenched the shard and drove it up into his throat. It wasn't a knife. She couldn't cut. She drew it out and plunged it again. And again. And again. Leverage was one thing; survival another.

The hand left her throat and went to his own, trying to staunch the spurting blood. His eyes, which had been hard, showed her his fear, and Mai pushed him off her. She stood over him, his blood dripping from her face, her hand, and she put the shard deep into his right eye.

"Not exactly a magic wand," she muttered, "but it'll do."

She relieved him of his gun and ammo and never hesitated to step across the threshold of the door. In her mind she heard the soft pops of clothes on a line, drying in the breeze, and she was free.

- 10 -

PRIZRAKI*

Directorate Headquarters, 1983

Taking advantage of Alexei's and Nelson's need to draw a breath, Mai Fisher asked, "May I say something?"

Both men looked at her, the set of Alexei's mouth and Nelson's frown showing their annoyance at the interruption.

"You've gone around and around on this, and you're getting nowhere," she said.

Alexei Bukharin leaned back in his chair and regarded her with something close to contempt. "By all means," he said, "if you have a suggestion..."

"There's no need for her to make a suggestion," Nelson said. "I'm firm on this. We're out of the Nazi-hunting business."

Alexei got up from his chair and paced the length of the conference room, his hands brushing back his hair.

Mai could hear him muttering under his breath in Russian, but she couldn't catch a word.

He turned back to glower at Nelson.

"I can't believe you've forgotten how much this means to me," Alexei said.

Nelson's scowl was as deep as Alexei's. "Don't you dare fall back on our friendship, Alexei. Right now, I'm your boss, and I've made a decision. The United Nations Intelligence Directorate has more important uses for our limited human assets than chasing down old men who were Nazis."

"And what's this organization's motto? In truth, justice; in justice, truth," Alexei said. "Where's the justice in giving up that hunt?"

P. A. DUNCAN

"It's someone else's job now, Alexei," Nelson said. His sigh was audible. "The FBI, Interpol, the Israelis, but not ours. This organization has indulged your desire for revenge long enough."

Alexei whirled and slammed a fist into the conference room wall.

Nelson took up his cane and pushed to his feet. He looked at Mai and canted his head. "Talk to him," he mouthed.

She rolled her eyes, but he nodded toward Alexei again and limped from the room. *Oh great*, she thought, *don't think I won't remember this.*

Mai went to the opposite end of the room where Alexei stood, his back to her. When she got close enough, she saw him cradling his right hand.

"Ah, I see you forgot that the walls of this room are steel-reinforced," she said.

He looked at her, eyes narrowed in warning.

"Here," she said, gentle in taking his hand in hers, "let me see if you've broken anything." She began to probe his fingers, hand, and wrist, noting the knuckles were scraped and the wall was unmarred. "I know how important this is to you, but..."

"You weren't even a gleam in your father's eye, Mai. You have no idea how important it is to me."

"My parents fought in the war, Alexei, and I'm a student of history, including yours. You hunt Nazis because they killed your father and two of your siblings."

"That was an unofficial part of the deal when I defected. I had leeway to pursue any war criminals I got intel on. It appears I should have insisted upon official."

"Like Nelson said, even if you stop, there are plenty of others who'll carry on."

"Nelson is a fucking sheep being herded by our former Nazi Secretary-General."

"Being in the Austrian Army didn't necessarily make him a Nazi," Mai said.

"The Army had to join the Party. He was a card-carrying Nazi."

"And you were a card-carrying Communist for how long?"

He jerked his hand away from her. "What the fuck does that have to do with anything?"

"I'm trying, unsuccessfully it seems, to point out to you that you need to pick your battles. Don't fight Nelson on this. Besides, what would you do? Quit and strike out on your own?"

He cocked his head to one side as he considered that, and she gave herself a mental kick for suggesting it.

"I'm sure Nelson would have something to say about that," she said, keeping her voice as neutral as possible.

"And you'd be the one to tell him, wouldn't you?" His eyes lost a little of his anger, and he said, "I need to do this. Nelson knows that." Alexei flopped down in a chair, put his elbows on the table, and dropped his forehead into his hands.

Mai sat in the chair next to him and moved it closer but made sure she wasn't touching him. She'd been his partner long enough to know when to touch and when not.

"How many former Nazis have you uncovered?" she asked him.

He raised his head and looked at her, frowning. "What?"

"Didn't you keep count?" she asked.

"Of course. Twenty-one."

"That's an impressive record."

"Mossad's is better."

"Well, yes. Mossad is an entire organization. You're one man, who has other responsibilities besides this 'unofficial' side work. Again, Nelson's right; it's not like people will give up looking for Nazis."

He rubbed his face again, covering it for a moment before he lowered his hands and looked at her. "You've met my mother," he said. She nodded, frowning herself as she wondered where he was headed. "Didn't you notice she never smiles?"

"My encounter with her was brief," Mai said. "She was pleasant."

"I didn't say she was unpleasant. She never smiles, and for as far back as I can remember, on every birthday I had, she wept. When you're five or six or ten or eighteen and all your birthday memories are of your mother crying over her dead husband and children, you have to do something."

"Were any of the Nazis you exposed at Stalingrad?" Mai asked. Alexei's father, brother, and sister had died in the Siege of Stalingrad. No bodies were ever found.

"I don't know, and I didn't care. A Nazi is a Nazi. Now or then."

"Some would say of you, a Communist is a Communist, now or then."

She saw none of his frustration had dissipated when he glared. "You keep bringing that up. What the fuck are you implying?"

"Nothing. It's another unsuccessful attempt to turn your words back on you."

"When will you learn?"

"I'm Irish and stubborn, and I'm trying to get you to give this up and accept Nelson's decision."

"What would you do if I asked you to ignore the fact the Taiwanese Secret Police killed your parents?"

"I'm not asking you to forget it, Alexei. I've accepted the fact there's nothing I can do about what happened to my parents and moved on. I'm asking you to do the same."

"It looks as if I have no choice. My oldest friend gives me orders. My partner—my wife—takes his side."

Of course, she was his "wife" when he was trying to score a point, and that pissed her off. She said, "You know, I've learned not to be affected anymore by your passive-aggression. Our work may not be as important to you as hunting Nazi war criminals, but it's important."

"Mai, we peek through keyholes and blackmail people. That's hardly the same."

"You've never had a problem with it before, Alexei. Why now?"

His eyes settled on a point across the room. He slumped in the chair, the rest of the fight leaving him. Without looking at her, he shrugged, telling her even he didn't know.

She knew. Alexei was many things—a spy, a remorseless killer when needed, a talented cook, her lover, and a man with a well-honed sense of justice. More than all that, he was a son, a fatherless son, who had struggled his entire life with the fact he was a constant reminder to his mother of what she'd lost. Of all his siblings, living and dead, he was the only one who resembled the late Nicholai Alexandreivitch Bukharin, the father who died serving Mother Russia when Alexei was still in the womb.

"There was one man," he said, jarring her from her reverie. "I was certain he was a guard at a *Russenlager*, an impromptu POW camp for Red Army soldiers. The intelligence I had said that he carried a die made from a Soviet soldier's bone. I stalked him for a week, made certain he knew someone was following him, watching him, hunting him. When I finally decided it was time to capture him, he hadn't slept for days. He wept and pleaded with me, swore he wasn't the one, but he was a lying, Nazi *svenya*, after all. So, I killed him, and I took the die for a trophy."

The face he gave her held more emotion than she'd ever seen him show. "I gave it to forensics," he said, and she had to strain to hear him. "They're working with Alan Jeffreys on using DNA to identify people. I had this silly thought that somehow they might eventually be able to identify the soldier the bone came from."

He must have seen her frown because he gave a hint of a smile. "I know it was impossible, but I thought since my mother had nothing to bury perhaps some other Russian mother might."

"What did they find out?" she asked, her voice as soft as his.

He looked at the palms of his hands, as if seeking something there. He clenched his hands into fists, and she heard him sniff. "It wasn't bone," he said. "It was ivory. The intel was wrong."

In the long silence that followed, Mai wanted to touch him but couldn't. It wasn't that she didn't know he'd killed. She was more than aware of it. She'd been around for some of it, and he'd taught her how to kill. The whole time, she'd assumed he'd killed only for justice, that every life he'd

56

taken deserved to end, that he was incapable of making a mistake about guilt or innocence.

"Nelson's right," he said. "It's time I stopped chasing the ghosts of my father's killers."

Mai swallowed, hard, several times, to make certain her voice didn't break when she spoke. "Yes, we have keyholes to peek through, people to blackmail," she said.

"Other wrongs to right," he murmured.

Alexei stood and held his hand out to her, and she didn't hesitate to take it.

Author's Note: The Nazis took almost six million Red Army soldiers (men and women) prisoner during World War II. Some sixty percent of those POWs died from deliberate starvation, exposure, or execution—up to three and a half million.

*"*Prizraki*" is the Russian word for "ghosts."

- 11 -

BOREDOM AND TERROR

The Middle East, 1984

"Well, this is about exciting as watching clothes dry," Alexei murmured, so only Mai could hear.

Mai smiled but didn't take her eyes away from the monitor, which showed two men having lunch—a very long lunch—at the hotel restaurant.

"You're upset we're not watching a swallow bait a honey trap," she said, her voice low as well. "You'd be sad if aliens invaded the earth and there was no sex involved."

"I thought that was why they came here." He was silent for a moment, but his eyes didn't leave the monitor either. "You do know the U.N. has alien first contact protocols."

"Yes, I do. I've read them from cover to cover—a little long on guessing but adaptable. I hope I'm the one who gets to execute those protocols."

"You know very well the leaders of the world would be so afraid of aliens that they'll simply lock them away and cover it up."

"I thought they already did that at Roswell."

Alexei's eyes slid to her, retort on his lips, but he saw her sidelong smile at him.

"Good one," he said. "Nice delivery. Very believable."

"Yes, I've been practicing. Oh, look, they've ordered another bottle of wine."

"Are you bored, now, too?"

"Yes, but at least I won't be constantly bemoaning it. I'm accustomed to it."

"What on earth do you mean?"

"It's not the company, I assure you. It's like flying, Alexei," Mai said, still no louder than a whisper. "Hours and hours of sheer boredom punctuated by moments of sheer terror."

Alexei gave a soft laugh, and whispered to her, "You realize, the next time I go flying with you, I'll remember the sheer terror remark."

"Always be nice to your pilot," she said, again smiling.

On the monitor they watched a third man come to the table and sit. He shook both men's hands and waved away the waiter who approached with a third wine glass.

Even though they knew the recorder was on, Mai and Alexei both glanced at it to make sure. Alexei unplugged the headset so they could hear the conversation as well.

"…you understand what the job is," the newcomer was saying.

The taller man of the two original diners nodded. Though the man used a variety of aliases, a practical and life-saving action in his line of work, Alexei had called him "Mutt."

In reply, Mutt said, "You have a pest in your home. You want it eliminated."

"Quietly and cleanly," the other diner said. He was much shorter than Mutt, and Alexei called him "Jeff." "You have the down-payment for our pest-removal services?"

"Yes, the agreed-upon amount, though that much cash was a little difficult to get."

Mutt said, "What can be transferred into a Swiss bank account can be transferred out. Cash is tangible. Do you want us to eliminate the pest at night when he's dormant?"

"Or do you want us to make an example for the other, possible vermin?" Jeff asked. Even on the monitor, the gleam in his eye was visible.

"I'm thinking that perhaps if it looked like a fight, it would be less suspicious. The pest has an abrasive personality. A fight would not be out of character."

"Too many variables," Mutt said.

"Too many witnesses," Jeff added. "I think it's best to make it a break-in, a home invasion."

"Yes," Mutt agreed, "all the pests can be eliminated that way."

"All the pests?" the third man asked, a tremor in his voice.

"It's always important to destroy the nest," Jeff said.

"Even the, uh, little pests?"

"Especially those. Leave them around, and they grow up and become a problem," Mutt said.

The third man at the table leaned back in his chair and glanced around the restaurant, his eyes skipping from table to table. It seemed at one point he looked directly at the camera, but that was coincidence. He took up a napkin and mopped his face.

Plotting someone's murder wasn't so casual after all, was it, Mai thought.

The man refolded the napkin and appeared to collect himself. "Yes," he said. "If you think that's the best approach…" He broke off and shrugged.

"Come on, come on," Alexei muttered. "Don't leave it there. Say it. Say it."

"Yes," the third man said, "all the pests must go."

Alexei sat back, fists clenched in triumph.

"No money has exchanged hands," Mai said. "Don't get too excited yet."

"A wise choice," Jeff said. "Our fee?"

"I have it here," the man said, patting a breast pocket. "Divided between two envelopes, as you requested. Fifty thousand American each now. Seventy-five thousand each after, but you didn't indicate how…"

"We will contact you with specifics about where you can drop the cash," said Mutt.

"And should there be any problem with the payment," Jeff said, "remember, we took out an insurance policy."

"Insurance policy?" the man said, his eyes darting back and forth between them. "What do you mean?"

"Best you don't know," Mutt said. "The fee?"

The third man took two envelopes from his inside jacket pocket and slid each across the table to its recipient.

Mutt pocketed his, but Jeff tore the envelope open and began to thumb through the bills.

"What are you doing?" the third man asked, his eyes again making a nervous circuit of the room.

"Counting the money," Jeff said. "My partner is the trusting one." Satisfied, he shoved the envelope into the side pocket of his jacket.

"Uh," the third man said, "when will… I mean, when will you…"

"Within forty-eight hours you'll receive a message from us like before, an ad in The Financial Times, telling you where and when to drop the money. Best you do it yourself."

"Of course, of course."

Mutt and Jeff stood, and the man looked at them with some surprise.

"Oh," Jeff said, "I assumed you'd be picking up the tab. Nice doing business with you."

Mutt and Jeff picked their overcoats up and began to put them on. Jeff did deliberately look into the camera and gave a wink before he and Mutt strolled away.

The man left at the table waved for a waiter, ordered a glass of wine after all, and asked for the table's check. When the waiter produced it then and there, he muttered under his breath about the amount but pulled out a credit card.

Alexei turned to the third person in the room. "Enough for you, Mr. Prime Minister?"

"The bastard is using his official credit card to pay for their lunch," the man said. "Yes, Mr. Bukharin, that is enough. Thank you for arranging this elaborate ruse, and your and Ms. Fisher's repartee is diverting if not amusing. Your operatives may keep the money."

The Prime Minister stood, his face lost in the shadows, and Mai and Alexei stood with him.

"I'm afraid that's against our ethics rules," Mai said.

The Prime Minister waved a hand at her. "Give it to some charity. You choose."

He went to the door and opened it. Two of his bodyguards entered. One carried what looked like a rifle case, but it was too wide for that. Mai looked at Alexei, who gave her an almost imperceptible shrug.

The Prime Minister said to them, "I need to make some arrangements. Can you return for your equipment in an hour?"

"Of course," Alexei said. His hand curled around Mai's elbow and gave a slight squeeze. She had been ready to speak, and he was telling her not now.

"Excellent. Please have a drink at the bar. On me."

"Thank you, Mr. Prime Minister. We'll do that," Alexei said. He urged Mai toward the door, and she waited until they were in the glass-walled elevator to speak.

"Alexei, what on earth..."

He walked to the rear of the elevator car and looked down at the lobby restaurant. It took him only a second to locate the man they'd taped plotting the murder of the Prime Minister, his political rival, and the Prime Minister's entire family.

Alexei's silence made Mai come to his side, and she followed his gaze from the man at the table to the room they'd left and back again.

"Alexei," she began again.

He once more lay a hand on her arm as he brought his eyes back to the man at the table as an arrow penetrated his heart and pinned him to the chair.

The wine glass crashed to the floor, and the momentum from the arrow tipped the chair backwards.

"What the fuck!" Mai said, her hands pressed against the wall of the elevator.

"Did you forget the Prime Minister was a gold-medalist archer for his country's Olympic team? Never mind the drink," Alexei said. "And the equipment. I'd like for us to be far from here when the police arrive."

By the time the elevator glided to a stop, people in the restaurant had surrounded the dead man, and he was lost from their view.

- 12 -

A STUDY IN BLUE

Egypt, 1984

"Alexei!" Mai shouted. "Hang with me. Come on, keep those attractive, blue eyes open."

He struggled to stay conscious. The pain in his right side should have focused him, but it was too tempting to fall away into oblivion.

And he'd do that if Mai would just shut up. He must have murmured something to that effect, because her lips were at his ear whispering, "No, I'm going to nag you into living, *darogoy*, so you might as well pay attention."

"How bad?" he asked.

"The bullet went through and through and, I hope, missed everything vital. You're bleeding like a stuck pig, as usual," she replied, and he noted, with some pride, her voice was calm, steady.

That's my girl, he thought, no hysterics for her.

"I'm a woman, not a girl, Alexei," she said, and he felt her hands press harder on his chest, trying to stop the flow of blood. He'd said that aloud, too. "Talk to me," she demanded.

"Sorry. Too busy dying."

"No, you're not. Talk to me."

"Ironic."

"What is?"

"It started here in Egypt. Ending here."

"It's not ending here, you ass. Talk to me. Since you brought it up, tell me the story."

Was he missing something while he was busy dying? What was she talking about? "What story?"

65

"The defection story."

"You know that."

"So, refresh my memory. There were pyramids, right? And moonlight?"

A smile replaced the pain on his face. "And a beautiful desert flower," he whispered.

"Of course, you'd remember her," Mai said, and he heard the sarcasm.

He forced his eyes to lock on her face. Yes, steady, calm, and something more. Concern. Worry.

He should tell her everything would be fine, that she was young and would find a new partner, a better husband, but he didn't have the strength for the words. He remembered something, and his fingers fumbled at his pocket.

"What?" Mai said. "What is it?"

"Inside pocket." To him, his voice sounded far away. He looked at Mai again but couldn't see her through the fog over his eyes. "Something for you. From the market."

The world went from grey to red, but he could still hear her voice telling him to wait, that help was coming. Black crept in around the edges of the red, but he managed to get his hand into his pocket, felt his fingers close around what he wanted.

He didn't remember pressing it into her hand.

The world spun when he opened his eyes, but he realized he was still while a ceiling fan whirled above him. The pale, green walls hinted where he was.

"There you are," came the soft voice from beside him.

Alexei turned his eyes in the direction of the sound and saw Mai, weary by the dark circles under her eyes, but stalwart. She smiled at him and blinked. He knew she hated to cry in front of him, but he could tell she'd done so while he was unconscious.

"I made it," he said, genuine surprise in his voice.

"Yes, eluded the Grim Reaper yet again," she said, but with a nervous laugh. "You need to trust me when I say help is on the way."

"Are you all right?" he asked her, after his eyes searched her form.

"Fine. Now."

"Get some rest," he said.

They had a silly compact between them. If one were hurt, the other stayed until the danger passed.

She sat on the side of the hospital bed and leaned down until her face was close. Now, that would be the image to carry into the afterlife—her expressive eyes and incredible smile—but apparently he'd hopped off the boat crossing the River Styx at some point.

"I'll be back after a few hours' sleep," she said. "Here's something you can remember me by." She kissed his dry lips as she wrapped his fingers around an object she placed in his hand.

"As if I could forget you," he said, and she laughed, her breath warm on his face.

"You never cease to dish the charm, do you?" she replied and kissed him again. Then, she was gone.

He may have dozed. He wasn't sure. You never were when you walked this close to the edge of death and survived. It took him a moment to realize his fingers clutched something small and hard. Though it was an effort to raise his hand to peer at what she'd placed there, it was an effort worth it.

He saw the small, lapis lazuli scarab set in a filigree brooch he'd spotted a few days before in a local antiquities shop. Probably ninety-nine percent of the so-called relics there were fake, but the brooch had caught his eye and made him think of how it would look nice pinned to Mai's blouse. He had intended to make a joke of it, tell her it would remind her of his eyes, but work and near-death had intervened. Yet, somehow he'd managed to give it to her.

She would infer things from that, things he wouldn't let himself acknowledge, but they'd deal with that later, as they always did.
Sleep pressed on him again, and he closed his fist around the scarab. His hand dropped to his chest, coincidentally over his heart.

- 13 -

THE ONE WHO GOT AWAY

Directorate Headquarters, 1985

Nelson's appealing features had twisted into something more than concern. "Can you confirm there are no survivors?" He spoke into the microphone that curved around his cheek.

"Affirmative, Chief, no survivors," came the agent's voice on the other end.

Nelson pulled off his headset, mussing his usually perfect hair, and threw it on his desk. His hand struck a stack of files, which slipped to the floor, their contents intermingling.

That made both Mai and Alexei turn toward him. Nelson grabbed his cane and levered himself to his feet. He lurched toward the entrance to his private quarters. Mai started to follow, but Alexei said, "Better to leave him alone when he's like this."

"Alexei?" came the agent's voice over the communications link. "Are you there?"

"Yes, Hassim, I'm here. Something came up, and Nelson had to break contact," Alexei said.

"I, I understand. Tell him I'm sorry about Inga Decourcey."

"I will. Can you confirm the perpetrators?"

"Yes, that should be no problem."

"Take care of it."

"Of course."

"Over and out."

Alexei removed his headset, stood up, and stretched. They'd been sitting a long while, listening live to the team picking through what had been a

Directorate satellite office in Beirut. The Druze bomb hadn't been a direct attack on The Directorate. The office chief and the half dozen agents stationed there happened to be using a building housing some offices of Geymayel's Kataeb.

"Who is Inga Decourcey to Nelson?" Mai asked.

"She is, was, the station chief in Beirut," Alexei replied.

"I know that. It's something more. He's lost other agents before and never blinked an eye."

"Well, Inga Decourcey, she was..." He searched for words and shrugged. "The one who got away."

"From Nelson?"

Alexei nodded and looked around. The communication techs had left, so he could speak freely. "They were involved when I defected. She had been one of the youngest French Resistance operatives in World War II and one of the original class of Directorate agents. She was a perfect match for him in every way."

"What happened?"

"She wanted to be an office chief in the Middle East. Being Nelson's wife wasn't in her plans."

"They were married?"

"He wanted to marry her. She didn't want to be tied down. So, she went to Jerusalem first, then Egypt and Jordan, then Lebanon."

"So, that explains his commitment issues."

"Perhaps."

"I've never heard him mention her except in a professional way."

"I don't think they saw much of each other afterwards. When he was injured on his and my last mission, she came and stayed at hospital with him, but they quarreled. That may have been the last time he saw her."

"Don't you think you should..."

"What?"

"See if he's all right."

Alexei shook his head as he walked to Nelson's desk. He picked up the folders and loose papers from the floor, sat behind the desk, and began to sort them.

"Why not?" she asked.

"I've known him long enough to know you don't want to be around when his evil twin comes out." He looked up from his work and saw the concern on her face. "He'll be fine. He compartmentalizes better than any of us."

"He's your only friend, Alexei. He's lost someone important to him, and you're being your usual cold, impersonal self."

"If he wanted company he would have said so. Leave it, Mai," he said, and went back to sorting the files.

"You, of all people, have the context to give him comfort," she said.

When he looked at her, he saw her reaction, a half-step backwards, which meant his expression did exactly what he wanted. Yes, he had the context, and damn her for reminding him he'd already buried one wife.

"I'm sure there's something you have to do, Mai," he said, in senior agent mode. She didn't like it, but she left.

When he entered the well-apportioned suite of rooms that served as his apartment, Nelson longed for a window where he could peer out into the night. He longed, as well, to be able to leave here, walk out in the world, breathe fresh air. He could do all those things, but the security arrangements involved rather ruined the purpose for escape.

The valet, a leftover from his predecessor, moved silently into the room and said, "You're in early, sir. Shall I have your dinner prepared?"

"No, Lofton, I don't feel much like eating tonight. Thank you. You can go home."

"Shall I make you a drink before I go? I'm sure you could use one."

Nelson marveled at the grapevine in his supposedly top secret organization. "Yes, Lofton, thank you."

When he was alone with half the Scotch in his stomach, he limped into his bedroom and to his dresser. From the bottom drawer, beneath a layer of undershirts, he took a box about the size of a large book. He tucked it under his arm, went back into the living area, and sat on the sofa. The box he lay on the coffee table, and he sipped the rest of his glass of Scotch as he stared at it.

His father had made the box from the wood of a cherry tree that had graced the yard of the old family farmhouse in Virginia. One summer when his father was courting the new schoolteacher in town, a bolt of lightning brought the ancient tree down. By way of proposing, Delmer Nelson had presented the cherry wood box to Marylou Foye for "keepsakes of our children." Inlaid in the top of the box was a heart, made appropriately from heart pine, with an arrow through it and the initials DN and MF, a rare, sentimental gesture from the farmboy who'd run away to become a merchant seaman in World War I. That had been the only time Delmer had left the state, not to mention the country. He'd come home, marked by war, and become the farmer his family had wanted him to be all along.

Nelson's mother and father thought he, their only child born ten years into their marriage when they were both forty, had been killed in the Korean War. The flag-draped coffin they buried in his hometown cemetery had someone else's burned corpse in it. That was back in the day when The Directorate recruited people and ended one existence for them to start another. The logistics of that became unsustainable, and The Directorate came to operate much like the CIA. Agents could have lives on the outside—unless, of course, you were in management.

When that change happened, he'd considered going to his parents with a story about having been held prisoner all those years, but his mother was already dying of cancer, and his father was lost in a past world where he didn't remember he had a wife and a son, much less a dead one. After his mother died, he visited his father whenever his schedule allowed it, pretending to be a social worker. Delmer never once recognized him, and Nelson was with him when he smiled and whispered, "Marylou," right before he died.

Nelson reached beneath his shirt and withdrew a key on a chain about his neck. He removed the chain, inserted the key into the heart-shaped lock on the box, and turned it. The lock he lay aside, and his hands rested on the box as he debated whether or not to open it.

He heard the door to his suite open and looked up when Alexei Bukharin entered, his tie loosened, the top button undone on his shirt, jacket over his shoulder. He nodded to Nelson's empty glass. "Want another?" he asked.

"Yeah. Pour one for yourself."

Alexei tossed his jacket on the opposite sofa, picked up the empty glass, and walked to the bar. When he returned with two glasses of generous portions of Scotch, Nelson still sat with his hands on the unopened box. Alexei set one glass next to Nelson's left hand and sat on the sofa across from him, on the edge of his seat, elbows on his knees as he rolled his glass between his hands.

"Mai was worried," he said.

Nelson laughed at that and sat back. "Funny, I don't see your wife with you."

Alexei leaned back as well. "I have an image to uphold apparently, one where I'm my 'usual cold, impersonal self.' What's in the box?"

"Things I shouldn't have. Things we're usually so careful about. Pictures."

"Of Inga?"

"Of Inga. Of me. Of Inga and me."

In a single, swift motion, he sat forward, opened the box, and scooped the photos from inside. He handed them to Alexei.

Alexei set his drink aside and took the pictures, shuffling through them. One was a black and white of Inga Decourcey in a 1950's style sundress. She leaned against a tree amid a bucolic background, a breeze lifting her blonde hair a little. Her smile was almost demure.

"France?" Alexei asked.

"Spain. We took a few days after a mission, played tourists. It was a few years before you defected."

"She was beautiful," Alexei said.

"She was."

"I never saw her any way except with her hair up in a bun and wearing those mannish pants suits."

Nelson's soft laugh was touched with sadness. "She thought they made her look serious," he said.

The next photo was a young Nelson. He mimicked an Elvis pose—hands in jeans pockets, cigarette dangling from a corner of his mouth, his hair slicked back to a ducktail. Alexei smiled, shook his head, and handed the photos back to Nelson, who put them face-down on the table.

"You've almost lost Mai twice," Nelson said.

Alexei drank Scotch and nodded. "I'm one up on her. She's keeping score for some reason."

"How did you..." Alexei waited, knowing he'd get the question out. "When you thought she might be gone, how did you feel?"

"Angry. I wanted to kill the man who shot her. One of those times, I did."

"No, I get that. I'm there. What did you feel, here?" He touched his chest.

Alexei drained his Scotch, hoping to hide his discomfort. "This is between us?" he asked Nelson.

"Of course. In here, we're two old friends having a drink."

"It's never that simple with you, but I'll take you at your word. What I felt was wrong for the business we're in. You know. You cannot let people get close because it's too easy to lose them. So, I felt a hole, one I didn't know I had, that she filled, fills. I keep her at arm's length with my indifference and other women, and one day she'll hate me for it. Right now, it works."

"When Inga refused my proposal and left, I put up walls. I use women, too, for a different reason, and, yeah, there's a hole, one that was always there. I thought, someday, she'll retire, and..."

Nelson broke off, his eyes blinking rapidly, and he drank Scotch.

"I put a team on tracking down which Druze group planted the bomb," Alexei said. "Hassim thinks he can get it pinned down to a specific person. I gave him the kill order."

"That won't bring her back."

"No, but you'll feel a hell of a lot better, my friend." Alexei reached out and flipped the photos over, with the one of Inga on the top. "Do you need company any longer?"

"No, Johnny Walker and I will have a lovely evening. Go home to your wife."

Alexei winced at the word, a word he rarely used in relation to Mai, though she was his wife, something he'd pushed for on impulse and often regretted and just as often savored. He rose, took up his jacket, and headed for the door.

"Alexei?"

He turned back to Nelson. "Yes?"

"You know, you're the brother I never had, so take some fraternal advice. Inga and I parted badly when she visited me in hospital. Do you know why?"

With a frown, he shrugged. "I figured you asked her to stay, and she said no again." Alexei frowned again when he saw the play of emotion on Nelson's face.

After a moment, Nelson said, "She wanted to stay, and I said no. She wanted to take care of me, and I didn't want her pity."

Alexei blinked in surprise at that news. "Nelson, it wasn't pity."

"Yes, fuck it, I know that. Now. I know that too late. I said no, and she went back to Lebanon, and she died there."

The photos in hand, Nelson took his cane and rose. At the gas fireplace, he switched it on and opened the glass doors. He lay the photos on one log, amid the flames and watched the fire, much as a terrorist bomb had, obliterate Inga Decourcey's face. He closed the doors and turned back to his friend.

"So, here's the advice," Nelson said.

"I was wondering."

"Don't wait until it's too late," he said, and limped toward his bedroom.

After the bedroom door closed, Alexei took from his pocket the one photo he'd palmed—a shot someone had taken of Nelson and Inga seated at a table at an outdoor café, plates of food, a bottle of wine, and two glasses on the table between them. They had both leaned toward each other until their heads touched, and they held hands and smiled at the camera.

He studied it and decided he would find a way to secure a picture of Mai. Alexei put the photo into the wooden box, closed it, and affixed the lock.

- 14 -

PATIENCE

Romania, 1986

A droning invaded her dreams. Mai lurched into consciousness and brought her gun up. She scanned the area. Trees. Brush. More trees. And a persistent bee, which flitted among the remains of her dinner.

She lowered her gun and shrugged from beneath her sleeping bag. The only thing worse than sleeping on the ground, she decided, was sleeping sitting up on the ground. After holstering the gun, she stood and stretched stiff muscles, swatted at the bee when it flew at her face.

A glance at the tent showed her the two figures still asleep inside. She looked up at the gray sky and noted the low clouds hovering at the treetops. The sun, now on the rise, would clear them away in no time. Now, if something would clear away the fog in her head. Napping wasn't the same as sleeping, and the fatigue was beginning to get to her. She couldn't let that happen.

Mai stretched again, took the trenching tool from her pack, and buried the remnants of the previous night's MREs, hers and her two companions'. She dug quietly, her ears tuned to the sounds of the forest, seeking a twig snapping beneath a boot, a murmur, foliage brushed aside, anything that would clue her someone had followed them. Nothing for three days. Two more days of walking, and they'd be in Yugoslavia, free and clear.

Then, she could go back for Alexei.

"I'm not arguing with you about this," Alexei Bukharin said. "Take Dr. Grasu and his wife to the rendezvous point. I'll buy you time to get there. I figure I can hold out five days, maybe six, with the *Securitate*, and you'll have that much of a head start. Now, go get ready."

Someone, probably their contact in Romania, had blown their mission to the *Securitate*, and the secret police were on their way to the professor's mountain retreat to arrest anyone they found.

"There has to be another way…" Mai said.

"No," Alexei said, cutting her off with a certain annoyance to his tone, "there isn't. I've looked at all the angles. The mission is to get Grasu to the west. He won't go without his wife, so…" Alexei shrugged and handed her his holstered gun.

Mai wouldn't take it. "What are you doing?" she asked.

"Look, they'll buy my story longer if I'm not armed." He handed the gun toward her again.

Though she hated to concede he was right, Mai took it and placed it in the military backpack that was growing heavier with everything Alexei decided she needed.

"I don't like this," she told him. "Not any aspect of it."

"I know you don't, and I appreciate it, but the mission is foremost. You know that."

Indeed she did, but she was already thinking, planning ahead. That she would come back for him was a given, as it was a given she wouldn't share that plan with him. He'd only try to dissuade her.

"That's it," she said. "I can't carry any more."

"All right," he said. "Stick to the roads we used to get here until you get to the tree I marked with the L to remind us which fork to take at the path in the next valley. Obliterate that mark before you start walking." He stopped, his eyes narrowing at her. "Mai, don't. Don't cry."

She shook her head. "I'm not crying," she said, wiping the evidence from her face. She took a step toward him.

"No," he said, his voice soft. He held up his hand. "If you touch me, it'll make this more difficult on both of us. Get the pack and go. Now."

"You're coming home," she said.

The smile he gave her was too wistful for Alexei, and she could read the regret in his eyes. Regret for what?

"One way or another," he said.

That he could be so damned flippant pissed her off. She shrugged into the pack and turned from him before new tears could come. She made it to the door before she heard him call her name. If she turned back, she knew she'd never leave, so she stopped and glanced over her shoulder.

"You deserved more than the little I was able to give you," he said. "I wanted you to know that. Understand that you mattered to me."

The strength of her own will surprised her when she managed to walk away.

A rustling sound that wasn't the wind among the leaves caught Mai's attention, and she had her hand on her gun again until she saw a figure crawl from the tent. A former bi-athlete in the Olympics, Mirela Yonescu was tall and still fit and carried her seven-month pregnancy with grace and ease. Of the three of them, she was handling the trek the best. Her husband, Emil Grasu, was an academic and a bit soft. Mai was exhausted and preoccupied but had decided a pregnant woman wouldn't get the best of her in a physical contest.

"How long before we start?" Mirela asked Mai.

"As soon as possible."

"Emil didn't sleep well."

"I know." Mai had heard the two whispering long after they should have slept, but she understood very little Romanian. She could extrapolate, though, and understand Grasu's concern about his wife's condition in any language.

"Could we give him an extra hour perhaps?" Mirela asked.

One additional hour that Alexei would have to fend off the *Securitate*'s interrogators. That brought an image to mind she didn't want to see.

"One hour. No more."

"*Multsumesk*," Mirela said.

"You're welcome."

Mirela went behind the fall of limbs that been their latrine and re-appeared a few moments later. Mai handed her a Wet Wipe from her dwindling supply and two granola bars. Mirela nodded her thanks as she settled on a log and took a quick drink from her canteen.

"What will happen to your partner?" she asked.

"It's your secret police," Mai said, her tone edged with anger. "You can figure it out."

"They won't kill him," Mirela said. "If they think he has value, they'll work a trade through diplomatic channels."

"They'll send him to the KGB," Mai said.

"Why would they do that?"

"Because he defected from the Soviet Union, twenty years ago."

"They won't know that, and certainly he won't tell them."

"Not at first. Interrogation can be…"

"What?"

"Persuasive." That brought the image to mind again, and Mai applied herself to her own granola bar, hoping Mirela get the hint to stay quiet. No such luck.

"Are you married?" Mirela asked.

"What?"

"Are you married?"

"Yes."

"What does he think of your work?"

"He trained me."

"Oh."

The silence came again for a while, long enough Mai felt her fatigue heighten. If they didn't get moving soon, she'd fall asleep.

"Your job," Mirela said, "I suppose you call them missions. Your mission was to get my husband out, not me. Am I right?"

"He was the one who caught our attention, yes."

"Your partner, he thought I was the one who alerted *Securitate*, didn't he?"

"And you still have me to convince that's not true."

Mirela frowned and brushed a tendril of hair from her face. "What if it is true?"

"Is that a confession?"

"No, not at all. What made you change your plans and bring me along?"

"You're here. Isn't that enough?"

"You are angry."

Was she kidding? "Of course, I'm angry. We left my partner behind to buy us some time. Someone betrayed us. That's worthy of anger."

"I'm sorry."

"For what?"

"For your partner, but I love my husband. I didn't want to lose him. You must understand that."

The absurdity made Mai laugh, a short bark that left Mirela frowning. "Change the subject," Mai said.

"Very well. What made you change your mind about bringing me?"

"Why is that important?"

"How do I know that once you get Emil across the border, you won't put a bullet in my head? How do I know whether you're using me to make sure he leaves with you?"

Mai dry-scrubbed her face, felt the grit beneath her eyelids, what felt like fur on her teeth. She smelled so bad she offended herself, and she was tired of being questioned.

"You're quite safe," Mai said, "unless I find out you are responsible for betraying us. If that's the case, I'll put you in a deep, dark cell somewhere until I find out Alexei's fate. So, you better hope you're right about a diplomatic exchange, because I'll do to you what the *Securitate* is likely doing to him right now."

Mirela chewed slowly, her eyes never leaving Mai. "It is him, isn't it? Your partner is your husband."

"He's my partner," Mai said and stood. She looked at her watch. "Be ready to move in twenty minutes. Wake up Grasu."

"You said an hour."

"I changed my mind."

He didn't look up when the door opened. He slouched in the chair, trying to relieve the pressure from the cord that bound his hands behind him. Hours, perhaps days ago, he'd begun to ignore the cold and the fact he was naked against it. The bruises he could see, the blood that had flowed told him he was still alive, and he had told them nothing, would tell them nothing.

He had no sense of time. He could have been here hours or days or weeks or months. After a while, the beatings ran together in his mind. He had bruises on his bruises. There'd be more, and he steeled himself for it; for he was beyond hurting now. Death was close, and that was a relief and a regret both.

Footsteps echoed in the room until Alexei Bukharin could see the highly polished boots in front of him. He heard the rasp of a match, its crackling flare, and he smelled the bitter smoke of a Turkish cigarette.

He brought an image of his wife to mind and waited. Patience was all he had left.

- 15 -

HERE, THERE BE DRAGONS

Yugoslavia, 1986

Edwin Terrell, Jr., hated Russians and not because they were the enemy in the Cold War he fought. It wasn't because he was CIA, and they were, well, other. He couldn't stand backward cultures.

So, he didn't bother to hide his sneer as he examined the parachutes Mai Fisher had obtained.

"Shall I get you a magnifying glass?" she asked him. "Perhaps a microscope?"

When her English accent went beyond lilting to snooty, he knew her patience wore thin. "Don't get a bee in your bonnet, Baby," he said. "If we're going to jump using these, I want to examine every thread…"

"We don't have the time."

He ignored her. He was aware of the time issue. It didn't mean he had to let it dictate his emotions. "What's this shit?" He held up the gray nylon to show the symbol on the parachute.

"It's a Dacian Draco," she said. "That means…"

"I took Latin, Baby. Why the fuck is there a dragon on my parachute?"

"For fierceness in battle."

"Christ, it looks like a dog with its tongue hanging out."

"Look, who the fuck cares?"

"I do. If I'm risking my American ass with a Russki parachute, why does it have to be one with a fucking dragon?"

She snatched the 'chute from his hands. "Go home," she said, eyes flinty. "I don't need this crap from you. I'll find someone else."

"Not as good as me."

"I'd settle for someone second rate who doesn't bitch about the equipment and call me 'Baby.' Go. Leave.

"Nope, I told you I'd help, so hand it over."

Christ, Terrell thought, a Russki parachute, now a Russki airplane. It sat, squat and damned big on rows of tires, lights out so their dark-adapted eyes would stay that way. He and Mai exited what passed for an operations building at the small, Yugoslavian airport, and, after he finished scrutinizing the airplane, he had to jog to catch up with Mai as she headed for the rear cargo ramp. Her smaller frame seemed weighed down by all the gear she carried—parachute, rifle, backpack—but she'd managed to get ahead of him.

"Slow down," he called to her.

She whirled on him, marching up to him with such intensity, he backed up a step. "We can't afford to slow down," she said. Her right forefinger punctuated each word with a fierce jab on his chest. "We need to go and now. Every second we delay…" Her voice caught, her eyes blinking rapidly.

"Don't lose it on me now, Baby."

Her voice was low, soft, barely able to be heard over the AN-124's engines. "I don't want him to die."

"And it won't do him any good if we rush and overlook something."

"Snake, we've checked everything three times. I did a pre-flight of the Condor myself."

"What 'condor?' Oh, this Russian piece of crap?"

"It's a tried and proven Soviet military aircraft."

"The Russkis built it, Baby. That's all that matters."

"Well, rein in the jingoism, Snake. It's one of the best aircraft I've ever seen, and I'm getting on it, and, eventually, with some help, I'm jumping out of it. Now, can you please move your ass so we can save my husband's life?"

"Who, by the way, is a Russki." She balled her hands into fists. It was more frustration than an intent to hit him, but he decided to back down. "Never mind. It's not the time for jokes."

She rolled her eyes. "God, finally!" She turned and strode into the Antonov, hands at her sides, but still fisted.

The Russians on board regarded him with a wariness equal to his own. He suspected the only reason he was here was because of Mai, and the only reason she was here was because of Alexei. That was an odd relationship. Not Mai and Alexei. He'd decided they were pretty much made for each other, even if Mai had come to him that time for validation sex. No, it was the whole Alexei defection/non-defection/defection thing that had always made him suspicious. He was by nature suspicious, but some things were obvious.

He and Mai had been relegated to the rear of the aircraft, and the airmen had erected a makeshift curtain across the span of the deck so he couldn't see what they carried. There were no seats back here, but the Russians had given Mai a crate to sit on. Him? Well, he got to stand or sit on his ass on the floor, which is what he did. He took consolation there was no place for the Russki airmen to sit, either.

Because she sat, Mai again looked small, almost fragile, an adjective he'd rarely attach to her. He saw her left hand clutching the cargo netting attached to the fuselage, as if she hung on for dear life.

When he rose, the Russians all shifted, not exactly taking a step forward but turning toward him, hands twitching toward their sidearms. Though he spoke the language quite well, he pointed to Mai, but their piggish eyes watched him cross the floor of the aircraft until he crouched at her side. They continued to watch him. He didn't need to turn and see. He felt the eyes on his back.

He switched on the transmitter in his helmet and motioned for her to do the same.

"What?" she asked.

"You okay?"

"Delightful. I'm about to jump out of a perfectly good airplane, in the bloody dark, over the bloody Carpathians. Just bloody delightful."

He gave her a smile. "It's no big deal, Baby. It's like falling down the stairs."

"I fell down the stairs once in that bloody great house of mine. Broke my bloody arm."

He almost smiled at the number of "bloody's" peppering her speech. "But, Baby, you've got a bloody Russki parachute with a bloody fucking dragon on it to slow you down." She managed a half-smile and a small twinkle in her eye. He glanced over his shoulder at the Russians, who were talking among themselves. "Look, I've got something that will make you feel as fearless as that fucking dragon," he told her.

Without waiting for an answer, he took a small vial from his vest and unscrewed the top. The top had a spoon attached, and he mimed scooping powder from the vial and inhaling it through one nostril with the other pinched shut. She shook her head.

"Once never hurt anybody," he said. "Look, you're spooked. You'll never admit it, but I can see it. When we get on the ground, I need you alert, focused." He held up the vial. "This will do that for us both."

With his help, she got half the cocaine in the vial up her nose, and she glanced almost with self-consciousness at the Russians.

"Don't worry what they think, Baby. You'll feel it in a minute."

Which was good, he decided, because it wasn't long before the Russian jumpmaster came over and told them to hook up. He showed them where to stand—just outside the joint for the ramp—and Terrell felt the whole plane shudder when the ramp started to open.

The jumpmaster hooked up as well and began to walk them to the edge of the ramp. When they stood inches away from total blackness, Terrell glanced at his watch. Fifteen seconds away from 0400. His and Mai's hands rested on their carabiners, ready to release them. The jumpmaster began to count backwards from ten.

"...*pyat, chetire, trie, dva, adin, prigat!*"

They jumped.

- 16 -

FOUR SECONDS

London, 1988

Mai Fisher blinked, unable to accept what she saw.

"Alexei," she murmured, "it's a bomb."

She thought she heard an intake of breath from him over the radio, but his voice was ever-calm when he said, "Get everyone out of there. Now."

"No. There's a gas main that runs under this row of buildings," she said. "It's a small bomb, but it's enough to puncture that main and send blocks of buildings up in flames."

"I'll contact Home Office. See which bomb squad is closest to…"

"Alexei!" she shouted. "I don't have time to draw you a picture. The bomb is ticking. This goes off in less than five minutes. Now, I need you to shut up and let me think."

To emphasize that, she took the earbud from her ear so she wouldn't have to listen to him. She doffed her jacket after taking her small flashlight from a pocket. She flicked the light on and leaned down close to the bomb to study it. Certainly not the biggest one she'd seen nor the most complex. One brick of Semtex, a fuse, and a stopwatch.

And wasn't it ironic that on her very first mission after recovering from a bomb of her own making she faced disarming one? Making and disarming bombs weren't her forte. The last one she built left a crater in the Irish countryside and scattered pieces of nine IRA soldiers over several hectares.

Yes, the bomb looked simplistic, but you could never be sure, especially when you'd only had rudimentary training in defusing the things. It appeared that if she disconnected the stopwatch, she could shut it down.

There was a logic to that. If the point was to ignite the gas lines and maximize the damage, a small, easily concealed bomb was the way to go.

Yet... You'd want something that couldn't be easily disarmed in the eventuality of someone's finding it in time to disarm it.

"Stop overthinking," she told herself and heard renewed buzzing from the discarded earpiece. Alexei could still hear her even if she'd cut her connection with him.

She straightened and wiped sweat from her lip. Her glance strayed to the shop window. Thousands of people strolled the streets in this, the commercial area of London, shopping, heading to lunch engagements, sightseeing.

An elderly couple strolled by, the man using a highly polished, ornate cane; the well-dressed woman had her arm through his. By chance the man looked Mai's way and gave her a smile and a nod.

Alexei wanted that. The two of them to grow old together. Somehow that had become meaningful to him, and, once, that had mattered to her as well. In the grand scheme of things, in the big picture of what their jobs entailed, such a wish seemed self-indulgent. A year ago she had almost died, and that had changed her. The surprise had been how easily she'd accepted the inevitability of her death, how she'd spoken no warning, knowing the bomb she'd made—to make sure forty pounds of plastic explosives would never get distributed to IRA cells—was ready to blow, how she'd welcomed the thought of oblivion.

Nor did it surprise now that attitude hadn't changed.

When she looked again at this IRA bomb, time seemed distended. The sweep hand on the stopwatch moved with impossible slowness, and she wondered if she watched the final seconds of her life. She took a deep breath, hoped she wasn't about to murder innocent people with another bomb, and reached for the stopwatch.

When Alexei threw open the shop door, the first thing he saw was Mai, bent over, both arms braced against a wall, and she panted as if she'd run a marathon. The second thing he saw was the disarmed bomb. His eyes on Mai, he heard the faint sound of sirens—the bomb squad he'd summoned anyway.

He raised his wrist and spoke into his mike. "The bomb is disarmed. Repeat, the bomb is disarmed," he said. "This is removal only."

He heard the approaching sirens stop and knew he had only a few moments alone with Mai. Alexei went to her, took her by both arms, and turned her to face him. For a moment he read disappointment on her face, but she recovered.

"I'm all right," she said. He felt her try to pull away, and his hands tightened on her arms.

"Why the fuck did you stay?" he asked, wanting to shake her and wanting to hold her. She'd have none of either action.

"Someone had to. I'm fine."

"I'm not," he said. "You scared the hell out of me, Mai."

"I knew what I was doing, Alexei. Do you doubt that?" She once more pulled against his grasp, and he released her, watching as she picked up her jacket and shrugged into it. "I had it completely under control," she said.

As she walked past him, she tossed him something, which he caught.

He looked at the object in the palm of his hand—the stopwatch from the bomb. That was the only thing it could be. He turned it over to see how close he'd come this time to losing her.

The image of the sweep hand burned into his memory, and he'd have it in his frequent nightmares. What he saw made this one of those instances where he hated her as much as he'd come to love her. Either she'd known exactly what to do or she'd had incredibly good luck. The luck of the Irish, you might say.

He placed the stopwatch atop the disarmed bomb, so the Home Office would have it for evidence. As he did so, he saw his fingers tremble.

- 17 -

JUDAS GOAT

Romania, 1989

The new videoconferencing system Nelson had invested in for Directorate field offices worked better than Alexei Bukharin had expected. A clear picture, he supposed, made up for the fact that Nelson's voice and his lip movements were a bit out of sync and reminded him of a Chinese kung fu movie dubbed in English. Considering that when he'd first joined The Directorate, spotty communications via telex or using often inaccessible encrypted phone lines had cost agents' lives, this technology was almost magic.

"Oh, did I wake you?" Nelson asked, when Mai and Alexei sat shoulder to shoulder before a computer in the Vienna field office. His smirk told them he knew exactly what he'd interrupted.

"No," Alexei said, "we were awake."

He made certain Nelson could discern the annoyance in his voice. After several weeks in East Berlin debriefing former Stasi following the fall of the Berlin Wall, he and Mai had come to a relatively quiet Vienna for a break and to write their report—and to have a decent bed for sleep and for other activities they'd had scant opportunity to indulge.

"Sorry to interrupt, but we have an emergency request from a head of state for an extraction," Nelson said.

They'd had a briefing upon arrival and had heard some talk in Germany of uprisings in Romania. Not much of a reach to assume Nicolae Ceausescu and his wife wanted saving from the pitchfork-waving crowds.

Alexei looked at Mai, and her expression echoed his. "You're joking," he said to Nelson. "You want us to risk our lives rescuing Ceausescu?"

89

"No, I want you to get in and make an on-site determination if we should grant his request."

"Oh, well, then," Mai said. "That's so easy."

"Nice to see your talent for sarcasm renewed," Nelson replied, but he sobered. "Look, Romania's so closed down right now we can't get a good assessment of the true situation. The few contacts we had there are suspiciously silent."

"That means going in blind," Mai said.

Alexei turned his head to her. "Nelson and I have some unofficial connections in the Romanian Army," he told her. "Not blind." He looked back to Nelson. "Near-sighted, perhaps."

Nelson's expression showed he agreed. He said, "Look, if it were left up to me, I'd let the Ceausescus go the way of Mussolini. Unfortunately, Perez de Cuellar doesn't want the decision to rest with one man."

Alexei considered an issue he didn't want to voice. Mai was still in a dark place after her capture and torture by the Stasi in the months before the Wall fell. The concern he felt wasn't for her capability but for the state of mind another foray into revolution might create.

Nelson was good at reading his old partner's nuanced expressions. "In and out. Forty-eight hours tops."

Most of the army still remained loyal to Ceausescu, and a half-dozen soldiers got Mai and Alexei inside Bucharest's Central Committee building. As she strode the corridors past broken windows, Mai caught glimpses of the crowds on the outside and hoped the soldiers would be as willing to see them safely out again.

Ceausescu's newly formed opposition had cut power to the building, and soldiers led Mai and Alexei up the stairs with flashlights showing the way. Halfway down a long, dim corridor, the soldiers stopped, and a colonel, if she read the Romanian insignia correctly, knocked on a locked door.

The colonel had a brief conversation with someone on the other side of the door, and as if reading her thoughts, Alexei murmured to her, "They're confirming the colonel's identity."

The door opened, and the colonel motioned them inside. Mai saw this had been a conference room of sorts. The long table had been pushed against one wall and was laden with remnants of half-eaten meals of sausage rolls and bread, now molding. That, plus the fact the people inside hadn't bathed for a few days, gave the room a rancid enough smell Mai had to mouth-breathe for a few moments until her nose grew accustomed to the odor.

Ceausescu didn't look like the strong dictator he often portrayed on state television. His clothes were disheveled, and he hadn't shaved in several days. Elena Ceausescu had her fur coat clutched tightly around her, a Tiffany diamond and silver brooch in the shape of a flower on the lapel. Where her husband's dismay was evident on his pale face, her defiance remained. Rather more than a little old lady, Mai remembered. When Ceausescu had gone on a recent state visit to Iran after the demonstrations started in Bucharest, he'd left his wife in charge of the military and the police. Without hesitation she'd ordered them both to fire on unarmed demonstrators.

Mai suspected the negotiations would be with her, and when the two women's eyes met, Mai's Irish came up. Elena Ceausescu was more than an ambitious woman; Mai's intuition told her the dictator's wife had an aura of evil about her.

The Ceausescus sat well away from the windows, side by side in large chairs, like rulers awaiting obeisance from peasants. On a small table between them sat a bottle of plum brandy and four paper cups.

"The soldiers must go," Alexei said in Russian.

Elena Ceausescu responded in the same language, "Why? So you can kill us?"

"No. I was sent here to negotiate with you, not them."

"Negotiate?" Elena asked. "You were sent here to bring us to safety."

"I came here to negotiate with Comrade Nicholae Ceausescu."

The old man's eyes left the floor and settled on Alexei. Mai saw a spark of arrogance still there. "Who are you?" Ceausescu asked.

"The soldiers have to leave," Alexei said.

Ceausescu gave a nod to the three soldiers in the room, and they filed outside and closed the door. "Now, who are you?" he asked.

"I'm Alexei N. Bukharin. This is my partner, Mai Fisher. You asked the U.N. for asylum. We're here to determine if the U.N. should grant that request."

"Show me your identification," said Elena.

"Madame Ceausescu, we're from the portion of the U.N. where carrying identification is problematic," Mai replied.

"I was wondering when you would speak," Elena said. "I thought perhaps you were one of those soft, Western capitalist women the men keep around for decoration."

Mai didn't rise to the bait. "When you were told we were coming, you received a code phrase, did you not?"

"Yes," said Elena.

"Iulie Teze," Mai said, having practiced the Romanian in Vienna to assure authentic pronunciation. July Theses, a long speech in 1971 where

Ceausescu had laid out his proposals for Romania's future as a Socialist Republic.

"Bring two chairs over," Elena said to Alexei. "We'll sit and 'negotiate.'"

When Mai and Alexei sat across from them, Elena poured plum brandy into the paper cups and handed them around.

"Noroc," Alexei said and drank his brandy down in one gulp. His fist crumpled the paper cup, and he tossed it over his shoulder.

Mai drank hers the same way, holding back her grimace, and almost smiled at Alexei's wishing the Ceausescus good luck.

"Now," Alexei said, "explain to me why the U.N. should expend resources to get you out of here."

"It is inhumane to leave us to the mob of sheep outside," Elena said.

"Sheep?" Alexei asked.

Elena waved her hand, dismissing his question.

"Answer," Mai said. This forcefulness was something new to her, and she found she took to it with a certain ease.

Elena looked at Mai again, with something of a smile on her face. "You have a bite," she said. "That is good in a woman, an admirable trait. They are sheep because they bleat only what they have heard from agitators. They follow anti-revolutionary students like sheep following a Judas Goat. They deserve what they will get."

"We need to re-group," Ceausescu said. "We leave the country for a while, the rabble will soon begin to starve, they will miss order and authority, and they will beg us to return."

"And when we do," Elena said, "we will need the help of your 'portion of the U.N.' to identify those who started this anti-revolutionary movement."

Mai inhaled a deep breath and wished she hadn't. The effluvium almost made her gag. She realized she now held these two elderly people in the same position where her Stasi interrogator had her a few months back. A decision from her, and the Ceausescus would find a safe haven and have access to the money embezzled from their supposed Socialist Republic. Another side of that decision was something too unpleasant to think about, but she did, having recently looked into an abyss herself.

She glanced at Alexei, their eyes connecting, communicating.

In English, he said, "I've heard enough."

"Yes, I have as well," she replied.

She rose and re-buttoned her coat. In Russian she said to the Ceausescus, "Thank you for the brandy."

Alexei led them to the door.

"Wait!" said Elena.

Alexei didn't turn at the sound of the voice, but squared his shoulders and stared at the door. Mai faced the Ceausescus again.

"You get back here!" Elena shouted, her face twisted, spittle flying. "You come back here and take us with you!"

"No," Mai said, calm, almost serene. "I think it's time to let the sheep in to graze."

In the corridor they could still hear the woman's ranting as they walked past the surprised soldiers. Alexei stopped by the colonel. "Do you have a helicopter you can use?" he asked.

"Yes," the colonel said, frowning.

"You need to get them out of here and soon," Alexei said and resumed his walk.

The military escort got Mai and Alexei beyond the raging crowd around the Central Committee building, and once they were in their rental car headed for the airport, Mai spoke.

"You told the army colonel to remove the Ceausescus," she said.

"I did, but when we get to the airport, I'm making a call to an old contact I have in the *Securitate* to let him know what's happening. They'll track the helicopter's route of flight, and things will take their expected course."

Mai's laugh was light. "So, the Ceausescus are now the sheep, and we are the…"

"We," he said, interrupting, "are going back to Vienna for a sumptuous hotel, decent food, and an old world Christmas celebration. The two of us."

"That sounds appealing."

"And it'll be even more appealing if we ignore any briefings and news reports until the new year."

She studied his profile, hard as stone, and welcomed his logic.

- 18 -

THE TORTOISE AND THE HARE

Las Vegas, Nevada, 1990

Clinton Ceron hung his suit in his work locker with care. He needed to get one more day of wear from it. After tomorrow, he had a four-day break, plenty of time for the hotel's dry cleaning service to freshen it. He centered the name badge over the pocket and let his fingers trace "C. Ceron, Concierge" engraved on the heavy, brass rectangle. To the left of his name, the etched pyramid representing the Luxor Hotel shone.

He had lived in Las Vegas his entire life, had worked his way from a groundskeeper at an off-the-strip casino to the Luxor's day concierge, and was proud of that accomplishment at the young age of thirty-two. If he couldn't find something in Vegas, it wasn't here to be found.

Satisfied the suit was safely tucked away, he closed his locker and affixed the lock.

At ten p.m., the employee section of the garage showed him nothing except cars. As usual, he'd stayed nearly two hours past the end of his shift, finishing up tasks he'd taken on during the day and transitioning the night concierge on any outstanding items. When he saw a man leaning against his BMW, he looked around, hoping for a maid or a busboy headed home early, but no such luck.

He smoothed his hair back, dabbed the sweat from his upper lip, and approached.

"C.C.," said the man Ceron recognized as Lefty Rosenthal's top enforcer, Joe "The Butcher" Merz.

"Joe," Ceron said. "What's up?"

"Your pay-up date is two days away."

"It's no problem. I'll have it."

"That's good to hear, C.C. So, I can tell the Boss he's getting his fifty K in two days?"

"Fifty thousand!" Ceron blurted, the sweat beading on his lip again. "It's forty thousand. Not fifty."

"Yeah, you know, interest, handling charges, late fees. That sort of thing. Adds up. You're not disputing the Boss, are you, C.C.?"

"No, no, no, but, well, Lefty told me I could pay in installments, Joe."

"Well, Lefty's the Boss, and he gets to change the terms. So, in two days I'm gonna need fifty thousand."

"Joe, there's no way I can…"

"Then, you need to lay off betting on football, C.C. The boss is a businessman, and that's all this is—business. No more negotiating, *capice*?"

"I'll do my best, Joe, but I don't see how I can… Look, I've raised thirty-five thousand, and I get paid tomorrow, and after my bills and all, I'll have five thousand to add to it. I can get you forty thousand in two days. Forty thousand, and I can have the other ten in a month."

Joe Merz was Ceron's height—5'8", 5'9"—but built like a bulldog. Merz closed a fist in Ceron's shirt and lifted him to his tiptoes.

"C.C., what did I say, huh? What was it?" He slammed Ceron against one of the support columns in the garage. "No more fucking negotiations."

Merz released Ceron and smoothed the man's shirt and jacket. "Are we clear?" Ceron could only nod. Merz tapped Ceron's cheeks with his palms, hard enough to leave them reddened. "Just in case, here's a little reminder."

Merz pulled something from his side pocket and held it up. Ceron's knees buckled when he recognized his daughter's favorite stuffed toy, and he braced himself by leaning against his car. Joe tucked the toy in Ceron's jacket pocket and again patted Ceron's cheeks.

"See ya in two days, C.C."

Ceron watched Joe disappear into the garage's shadows. When he was sure his legs would hold him up, he fumbled for his keys and opened the driver-side door. He sat sideways, bent over, his head in his hands.

Mai Fisher had long accepted she and Alexei were actors in a play written by faceless, nameless men. At one time, that had dismayed her and made her question her chosen work, but she'd gotten over that drama. From across the garage, she'd watched the interplay between the concierge and the mob enforcer. Now, that was drama, but drama she could use.

She could have put a stop to it and let the mob guy limp away with bruised balls, but the fear he instilled in Clinton Ceron was fear she didn't have to manufacture. In fact, it put her in the position of being Ceron's savior, and men who needed saving would do most anything for salvation.

She brought her wrist up to her mouth and spoke into the mic there: "Get ready to move. I'm headed in."

Alexei's "Roger" was clipped, and she heard the muffled sound of the van starting on the other side of the garage. She pushed off the wall she'd leaned against and, with silent steps, crossed the expanse to the concierge's car. It took him a moment to realize she stood there, and when he did, he jumped, a hand going to his throat.

"Mr. Ceron," Mai said, "we need to talk."

"Wh-who are you?"

"A potential friend." She heard the van pull up behind her and stop. "If you'd step inside here..." She pointed to the van.

"Look, if you're from Lefty, I just talked to Joe Merz."

"I don't work for Lefty Rosenthal. Mr. Ceron, if you don't get into the van, I'll put you in it, and I'll leave bruises."

All the suaveness he employed for his job disappeared. "No, I ain't going fucking nowhere but home."

"Mr. Ceron, I can help you."

Ceron gave a snort of a laugh. "The only way you can help me, lady, is if you got fifty thousand cash in your van. Now, leave me alone. I gotta figure things out."

"Actually, Mr. Ceron, the fifty thousand is not a problem, but I'll expect something in return," Mai said.

He stood up from the driver's seat, a spark of anger in his eyes. "Lady, this ain't something you can fuck with me about."

"I'm not. Step inside the van, and we'll go for a little drive and discuss your financial situation and how I can help."

Mai strode to the van and opened the sliding door. She watched Ceron crane his neck to peer inside. He shook his head and stepped closer to his car.

"No, no, I ain't getting in there," he said.

"In two days, Lefty Rosenthal wants fifty thousand dollars from you, fifty thousand dollars you don't have," Mai said, her tone calm, conversational. "You know the bank account where you stash your tips, the one you were going to use to pay off your gambling debt to Rosenthal? We froze that this morning. National security. So, you can't withdraw the funds."

"What are you? A cop?"

"No, but I'm in a position to be your best friend, a friend who happens to have the solution to your problem." After several mute moments, Mai added, "Joe 'The Butcher' Merz won't buy the frozen assets story. He'll think you've gone to the authorities, and you know he won't go after you. He needs you to pay up. He'll go after your children."

"Mai," came Alexei's voice through the receiver in her ear, "enough talk. Get him in the van now."

From her pocket Mai palmed a device resembling an Epi-pen, but rather than a life-saving dose of epinephrine, this hypo held a fast-acting sedative. A half-dozen strides later, she jammed it against Ceron's neck and caught him as he crumpled. Alexei was beside her, taking up the man's feet. Their burden between them, they stowed Clinton Ceron in the back of their van and climbed into the front seat.

Behind the steering wheel, Edwin Terrell, Jr.'s eyes swept the area before he drove away.

"You do know," he said to Mai, sandwiched between him and Alexei, "at the CIA our code name for you is 'Tortoise.'"

"Slow and steady wins the race," Mai said.

"We haven't crossed the finish line yet," Terrell said. He stopped at the garage's exit and showed a pass to the attendant. The gate rose, and he turned right, merging into the flow of traffic.

"Trust me," Mai said.

Terrell laughed and headed away from the bright lights of the Vegas Strip. "Famous last words."

Mai thought the Luxor hotel in Las Vegas the most unique feature of the city's skyline. Even from the airport it loomed over everything, and yet the pyramid it copied in Giza was much more massive. When she emerged from the limo, the black face of the Luxor soared, and the scale seemed exaggerated.

Alexei and Terrell came to her side and stood ahead of her, befitting the role of bodyguards. Clinton Ceron awaited them, and she could see a sheen of sweat on his face. That, however, could be from the ungodly heat rather than nerves.

Because she was the VIP, Ceron, back into his smooth and sophisticated concierge role, escorted her and her two "bodyguards" to her suite. As she tipped him, he slipped the two key cards she'd requested into her hand. Those disappeared into her pocket as she looked over the bags, which had been delivered to the room.

"Mr. Ceron, the small, black briefcase there isn't mine," Mai said. "Could you see that it gets to whom it belongs?"

Relief flooded the man's face, but he managed not to grab the case, which contained his money.

"My apologies, Madam," Ceron said. "I'll see that it's taken care of. Will there be anything else?"

"No, thank you, but I'll page you if I require something."

After Ceron left, briefcase in hand, the three changed clothes—Terrell into a tux, Mai and Alexei into casual black outfits perfect for a break-in but not full tactical. That would draw too much attention.

Terrell rubbed his hands together. "Well, since it's against the law for me to do what you're about to do in this great country, I'll go gamble with our mark while you bug his suite. Have fun, but try to be the hare this time," he said, and blew Mai a kiss before he left the suite.

"Ready to go?" Alexei asked.

Mai held up a room key card and the one for the inclinator. The shape of the Luxor made elevators impractical, but only the inclinator operators had keys to operate the devices. That had become policy when a tourist, bereft after losing his life's savings, had taken the inclinator to the top floor and swan-dived thirty stories from the walkway to the lobby below. Thanks to Ceron, they not only had a key card but an out-of-service sign on one inclinator so they'd have exclusive use of it for the next couple of hours.

Mai replied, "Ready as I'll ever be for climbing up an elevator shaft, or in this case, an inclinator shaft. Despite what the CIA wants, I'm taking that one step at a time."

Alexei grinned as he pulled on leather gloves. "Slow and steady bugs the diplomat's Las Vegas suite," he said.

Mai laughed with him and tucked the key cards in a pocket. Small flashlight in hand, she followed Alexei to the door of their suite.

What she'd done to Ceron, though certainly a lot less distasteful than what Lefty Rosenthal had in mind, hadn't brought her much pleasure. Now, breaking and entering with no one's being the wiser? That was much more fun.

- 19 -

LET IT GO FOR NOW

Bosnia, 1995

S omewhere a baby wailed. If the mother didn't hush it, the Serb paramilitaries would seek the mother out, poke and probe at the baby to determine its sex. Mai Fisher hoped the child was a girl. The Serbs would consider a Muslim infant boy a potential terrorist.

The mother must have known as well. The child's crying stopped, and in her periphery, Mai saw other women shift and press together to hide the mother and child. She kept her eyes straight ahead, at a spot in the distance and away from the crowd of men and boys. She'd tried to count the males as the Serbs separated them but gave up at 2,000, and now there were likely four times more.

Beside her, Alexei Bukharin was as still as a stone wall, and she leaned against him for assurance. He leaned into her as well, and they held each other up that way, gave each other strength.

Mai wondered how the Dutch Peacekeepers would explain the presence of two Russians and a Brit among them. The U.N. Observer title went a long way, but not with Serbs who knew better. This was a situation she had a specific familiarity with, being at the behest of peacekeepers who would consider their lives over those of spies. The last time didn't work out so well for her, and she'd become a Balkan warlord's hostage for eighty-seven days and fourteen hours.

Considering the spinelessness of the Dutch colonel—he'd all but opened the gates to the paramilitaries—she hoped the Serbs would find a reason to rough him up. The thought of it made her smile, and Alexei nudged her. She glanced to her left and saw the question in his raised eyebrow—what's so funny?

Mai sobered and shook her head, her gaze returning to the scene before her: men and boys separated from women and girls by the length of an American football field. Between the two groups the paramilitaries milled, clad in a mix of Serb army camouflage and jogging suits. They brandished their assault rifles and grenade launchers while they smoked and laughed, and she understood enough of the language to hear the taunts they tossed at the men. A unit of the regular Serb Army surrounded the compound, outside its flimsy chain-link fence, and they stayed there, as if to impart to any observer—or three—that what might happen inside the compound was not their responsibility.

A half-dozen of the paramilitaries approached a knot of women and held up German marks, trying to get some of the younger ones to dance for money. One girl, perhaps fourteen, stepped forward, and began to dance the *kolo*. The men clapped to encourage her, one joined her, and, after pressing the money into her hand, he led her away, behind a cluster of mismatched military vehicles. His comrades laughed and followed.

Mai felt Alexei's fingers encircle her wrist, almost too tight for comfort.

"Let it go," he murmured, his lips barely moving. "Let it go for now."

To her right, she saw Kolya Antonov's spine stiffen, and Alexei raised his voice enough for his nephew to hear. Again, he said, "Let it go."

The Dutch soldiers at least had the decency to look away as a soft sobbing cut through the tension—the girl's mother, no doubt, facing the loss of a husband, maybe a son, now a daughter.

As the afternoon wore on under the unrelenting sun, the girl who'd gone with the men reappeared, her knees scraped raw, her eyes showing sanity hung only by its fingertips. The top of her cotton blouse had but a small tear, but her skirt was askew, the zipper, which should have been in the back, now to one side. Her steps were slow, and as she neared Mai saw the blood that had run down her thighs and shins to stain the white, ankle socks she wore. One shoe was missing somewhere, and when she approached the women, most of them gave her their backs.

Alexei's fingers, which had never left her wrist, tightened again, anticipating, perhaps, she was as angry with the women—whose religion taught the girl was now a whore—as she was with the brutes who had lured her to defilement. Mai lost sight of the girl in the press of women and clenched her fists in frustration.

She hated this—being unable to act. Never mind she, Alexei, and Kolya would be three against several thousand Serb soldiers and irregulars; the 400-man Dutch contingent was outgunned as well. What she couldn't forgive was the Dutch let the nearly 30,000 refugees from Srebrenica into their compound but didn't protect them when the Serb Army and the paramilitary unit known as the Scorpions showed up and forced themselves inside as well.

When the Scorpions began separating the sexes, angry men and women had engulfed them, a vulnerable time the Dutch could have taken advantage of, but they hadn't. A regular Serb soldier had fired into the crowd, and when the mass of humanity pulled away like a single wave from shore, a dozen bodies lay in the dust. They lay there still, clouds of flies around each, the flies' drone the only sound now in the compound beyond the occasional sob from a woman or a shout from a soldier.

For the rest of the day, into the night, large buses, like those used for tourist excursions, came empty and left full. The men and boys shuffled onto them, filled the seats, and stood in the aisles. When the loaded buses fired their engines, a Serb soldier unlocked a padlock and opened the gate to let the buses exit. They drove straight ahead, turned right, and were lost from sight. The women waved even after they could no longer see the buses.

When the bus drivers had hauled the last man and boy away, never to be seen again, the Scorpians climbed back into their trucks and surplus army transports and also drove away, the Serb Army unit right behind him. The Dutch soldiers dispersed, and the women surrounded them, hands clasped in supplication.

Mai, Alexei, and Kolya watched the Serbs drive down the same road as the buses had. Mai willed the column to turn left, to head back to Srebrenica. She held onto the thread of hope that General Mladic's words were his bond, that the men and boys were only going somewhere to receive medicine, food, and water and that the women would join them soon.

She held onto that thread even though experience told her the futility of it. What hope she had left bled into the dirt when the military column turned right as well.

- 20 -

CLEOPATRA'S BARGE

Federal Penitentiary
Terre Haute, Indiana, 2000

A finger marking his place, John Thomas Carroll closed his battered copy of H.L. Mencken's *On Politics* when the guard called him to the door of his cell. Though it was well past lights-out time, he had earned points for good behavior and could stay up late and read.

Nothing official; merely, the granting or restricting of privileges informally arranged with the guards. Good behavior meant extra privileges, like getting to toss a baseball with a guard during his one hour of exercise a day. Bad behavior meant the loss of those few perks you had. A simple lesson he hadn't learned from experience; he was a good observer.

Given that, the guard's mood on a particular shift, even the guard him- or herself, could mean something you got to do yesterday you couldn't do today, and the official aspect of the federal prison system was understandably more bureaucratic about the privileges granted. Carroll supposed some shrink somewhere had outlined it, but there was no logic to it. First, he could use a ballpoint pen for his letters, but they controlled how many sheets of paper he could have. Without explanation, he would get a whole ream of paper, but the guards took the pen away in favor of a pencil. When he'd worn the point down on the pencil, a guard took it away for sharpening. Someone must have decided that put the pencil—all two inches of it—into potential weapon territory, and he got the pen back. But he had to check it in and out with the guard, who always inspected it to make certain he hadn't removed the innards, another possible weapon.

He never let them see how he felt about the capriciousness of it. He'd been brought up to respect authority, and nothing among the recent events of his life had changed that. From day one he had been no trouble, received not a single disciplinary action. The guards often referred to him as a model prisoner when chastising another inmate.

Tonight, as usual, he didn't break with his routine and make the guard wait. He put his book aside and went to the door. "Yes, sir?" he said through the grille.

"You've got a visitor. Put your hands in the slot."

Once his hands were cuffed, he stepped back. The protocol was more than familiar to him after almost a half-dozen years behind bars. Three guards—one to deal with the doors, one to put on the shackles, and one to keep a shotgun on him at all times—came into the cell, and he asked, "Sir, could I shave first?"

"It's not her. It's some guy," answered the guard he recognized as the shift commander.

"Not one of my lawyers?"

"No."

"Then who…"

"All I know is he's got permission from the attorney general to see you. I'm just the messenger boy. You can refuse, of course, since this is out of the ordinary, and your attorney isn't involved, but I recognize the guy. He comes with your friend, but he stays out in the waiting area when she goes in to see you."

Carroll hesitated at meeting a stranger in the middle of the night, but if he was associated with Siobhan… Why hadn't Siobhan come herself? Why was someone she knew coming instead?

He must have paled because one guard asked, "You all right, man?"

"Yeah, yeah, I guess so. I'll see this guy, and sorry for the inconvenience."

"No prob. It's a full moon tonight. Weird stuff always happens. Stand still for the shackles."

The four of them—him, a guard in front, a guard at his side, and a guard behind—wended their way through the corridors to the interview room. Outside the room, the guards usually took off his cuffs and shackles, but they didn't this time. He didn't question it, but one of them noticed his confusion.

"Your friend's the one who threatens to sue us five ways to Sundays if we don't uncuff you, but this guy's not her."

"Yes, sir."

"We're watching, remember?"

"Yes, sir."

The guard opened the door, and, hampered by the leg shackles, Carroll shuffled inside.

The man in the room was tall, over six feet, and he had a shock of white hair and piercing blue eyes. Carroll thought perhaps he'd seen him somewhere, but exactly where and when eluded him. Expressionless, the man looked him over and pointed to a chair. Carroll bristled a bit. This guy wasn't a guard, and it was one thing to know you had to do what they said. Regardless, he didn't act on the impulse to mouth off at the man. After all, the guards were watching.

He shuffled over to the chair, which had a table in front of it, and sat down. The man sat across from him and fixed him with an intense stare. Carroll guessed he was in his mid-fifties, and he was dressed well but casual, with a turtleneck sweater beneath the jacket. He wore a pricey watch but no other jewelry.

"You've put on weight," the man said. He had a slight accent, but Carroll didn't know what language.

"Begging your pardon, but how would you know?"

"I know."

"The guards tell me you've been here before with Siobhan. Where is she?"

"Not here. This conversation is between you and me, and if you ever mention it to her, your sister will meet with an unfortunate accident."

Anger flared in Carroll, reddening his cheeks, but he again remembered the guards. The man's flat, dead stare continued, and Carroll returned it in the same manner.

"My sister's got nothing to do with this," he said.

"And I wish my wife had nothing to do with it, either."

"Your wife? Siobhan's your... Oh."

Siobhan had told him that, and he'd put it from his mind, much as he had her real name. To him she would always be Siobhan, not Mai Fisher. All the while they'd been together, she was married. Even the night when it was obvious they were going to make love, she was married. She had also told him most of what they'd been to each other hadn't been a lie, but lying was part of her job. She was a spy.

"Is she okay?" Carroll asked.

"Physically fine. Mentally, she sinks lower every time she comes here."

"I told her to stay away."

"You left it up to her, and she will always choose to come."

"It's a free country."

"Now, that borders on ironic coming from you."

"Why? I'm the pro-freedom, anti-government guy who blows up buildings as an expression of free speech."

The man almost smiled. "She taught you sarcasm."

107

"Why are you here? Are you jealous of a dead man?"

"You're not dead."

"I can measure my life in terms of months and weeks."

The man considered that and shrugged. "I'm not jealous—anymore. I was at first because she and I were on a rough patch during that mission, but we got past it. And, frankly, as a lover, you'd never compare."

"I guess that would be up to her to determine. So, not jealous. Why are you here?" Carroll asked again.

"Do you know why she comes to visit you?"

"She promised she would. She keeps her promises."

The man shook his head. "She feels responsible. She feels she put you here."

"I put myself here."

"You know that, and I know that, but Mai still takes frequent trips on Cleopatra's barge."

For a moment, Carroll was nonplussed, but he soon got it. Cleopatra's barge on the Nile, as in *de-nial*.

"Look, Mister Fisher, I guess it is, since that's her real name…"

"My name isn't Fisher, and knowing my name is really of little use to you."

"Whatever. I've told her she had nothing to do with the fact I did what I did. She thinks if she'd fucked me, I wouldn't have. But I would have. I'd have made love her to every day I was with her, and I still would have done what I did. The only way she could have stopped me was the one thing she couldn't do."

"Kill you in cold blood. Yes, I'm aware. Too damn bad for the people in the building you blew up I didn't get to you first."

"Why didn't you?"

"I let the personal interfere with what I should have done. I dropped the ball. Not her."

Carroll's throat tightened at the memory of something Siobhan—Mai Fisher—had told him. "She told me, you know, who she…" Mindful the guards listened, he broke off.

The man's eyes narrowed at him. "She told you about that?"

Carroll nodded and inclined his head toward the door, where the guards watched and listened.

"You could have used that information to your advantage."

"Man, you don't get it. I wouldn't have done that. Siobhan was only doing her job. Yeah, at first I felt betrayed, but I've had time to think. I understand what she was trying to do. You know, if she'd hauled me in and told me what it was she was up to, I probably would have backed off. One thing I can deal with is honesty."

The man stayed silent, but his expression eased, his eyes shifting from a translucent blue to a deeper shade. "Let's not tell her that," he said.

"That there was another way to stop me? I'd never do that to her. Look, I can see you don't like me, I can understand that, but we have something in common."

"We both care for the same woman," the man said.

"Yeah, but you got it in spades over me. One, you'll live a lot longer. Two, you get to touch her."

"Three, I was there first."

"I thought you weren't jealous anymore."

"I'm a man. She's my woman."

Carroll grinned for the first time. "She'd be pissed as hell to hear you say that."

"Tell me something I don't know."

"Here's what you need to know," Carroll said. "I saw right away she could mean something to me. Any other chick at a gun show, I'd have nailed and walked away. But she saved me. Not long after I met her, I wanted to kill myself, and what stopped me was remembering her and the fact she said she wanted to see me again. So, yeah, lucky for me you didn't get to me first, but no one would have gone through any of this if I'd have pulled the trigger on myself seven years ago. Not my family, but especially not Siobhan."

"Her name is Mai."

"That's your woman. Siobhan's mine. So, look, it's late. You came here, threw some weight around, marked your territory. What exactly was the point?"

To Carroll's surprise, the man laughed with genuine humor. "You really have learned a thing or two from her. Those could have been her words," he said. He sobered, not with the anger he'd broadcast before, but real solemnity. "You want to know why I'm here. She and I have a piece of information about what happened at Waco on April 19, 1993, that could turn everyone's perception upside down. She wants to use that information to save your life."

"No. Tell her no." The man arched an eyebrow bisected by a scar. "Yeah, right," Carroll said. "No is not exactly in her vocabulary. Don't get me wrong, there are some things I'd give anything to do again—like, climb this tree in my Dad's backyard. I dream about that fucking tree, even though he lives in a different house and the people who bought the old house cut it down. And there are things I never did I regret I didn't do, like, of all things, fishing. I'd like to go golfing with my Dad. He always wanted me to, and I brushed him off. None of that changes anything about what's going to happen to me, and, deep down, she knows I'm not worth it. Remind her of that."

"That'll do no good," the man said. "She promised you wouldn't die alone, and she won't go back on her word." The man sighed and dry-washed his face, and Carroll saw the smudges of fatigue beneath the man's eyes. "I've kept us both up tonight for no reason. It's just that... I want her back."

Carroll looked around and laughed. "Man, this may be a bolt out of the blue to you, but I don't have her."

"Part of her is always here, with you, and will be even after you die."

"I don't know what to say to you. I've already said I told her I won't hold her to that promise." The man said nothing. "So, uh, can you tell me what the information is about Waco?" The man narrowed his eyes again. "I'm not going to tell anybody. I'm willing to see this through, you know, 'cause if my death can give people peace..."

"A false peace. They'll watch you die and feel cheated. Surely, you know that."

"I know it, but even if they're happy I croaked..." He broke off with a shrug again. "So, could I have a little satisfaction that maybe what I did wasn't all in vain?"

"It was completely in vain," the man said, and continued, "After the FBI assault at Waco, Mai found two shell casings in the FBI's sniper nest."

"Yeah, so? I've always thought the FBI shot into the building."

"The shell casings are of a particular caliber and manufacture used only by military snipers."

Carroll sat back in his chair as if shoved. "And you've been sitting on that all this time?"

"At the right time and for the right reason, it will come out. I hope you'll agree it's bigger than one man's life."

Since he'd been in prison Carroll had come to realize there were some things, a lot of things, really, far more important than his continued existence. When the government killed him, it would end his pain, which had never abated and for which he'd be more than grateful, and maybe it would fulfill the nation's lust for his blood. He nodded, a slight incline of his head, and he saw the man show a little surprise.

"So, I bet she doesn't know you're here. Man, you're in trouble," Carroll said.

The man's smile came again. When it did he seemed almost human. Of course, people had said the same thing about Carroll. The man stood up, but Carroll sat still. That was the protocol until the guards came in to take him back to his cell.

"I won't wish you luck," the man said. "That would be cruel and whereas I can dish it when it's needed, I'm not a particularly cruel man."

"You'll take care of her? I mean, without ever letting her know it," Carroll said.

"That's what I live for. I noticed that in all your regrets, you don't regret killing those people."

"Do you?" Carroll asked.

"What makes you think I've killed?" the man responded.

"It's written all over you, man."

The man shrugged. "You didn't like it, did you, when you killed, either time?"

"Both times were war in my eyes, and people die in war, but, no, I didn't like it, either time."

"I did, and I don't fall back on war as my excuse."

"And they call me a sociopath."

Another humorless smile crossed the man's face. "That's the essential difference between you and me, and why Mai is with me. She's always had a weakness for the dark side of men. She could have married someone dull and commonplace and lived a comfortable life of society parties, but she opted for an unusual occupation, an abnormal marriage, and to plumb the darkness in everyone's soul. You see, you weren't bad enough for her."

"I always suspected it was the other way around. Do you deserve her?"

"Probably not."

Carroll could read emotion in the man's eyes at last, an emotion he didn't want. Pity. "Look," Carroll said, sighing, "can I, like, go back to bed and never have to see you again?"

The man inclined his head but said nothing. He headed for the door.

Carroll looked over his shoulder. "I hope she makes you sleep on the couch for a week," he said.

"She never lets me off that easy," the man replied. "Die like a man."

Later, on his cot, lights out at last, he stared at the dark ceiling above him for most of the night. If there were a just God, he'd close his eyes right now and never wake up, never see Siobhan again, never look on someone he could never have. Death was the one sure thing in his life right now. No doubts or questions, no wondering about how or when. He knew, and that was powerful. He was finally in control of a haywire life. That was the irony, and he could appreciate it and savor it. No regrets.

Except for the one thing that had eluded him in his short, unhappy life. As sick as it was, what Siobhan had with the killer she was married to was better than anything he could have offered her.

And that erased his last doubt.

- 21 -

YEA, THOUGH I WALK

Former Republic of Yugoslavia, 2000

Mai Fisher belly-crawled to the top of the hill and brought the binoculars to her eyes. A scan of the ridges and valleys below her showed her she and Alexei were still alone. She glanced back over her shoulder and saw Alexei up to his waist in the hole he'd dug. On a tarp beside the hole, a pyramid of loose earth grew with each toss of his shovel.

Let it be empty, she thought. For once, let it be a wild goose chase. She stopped watching him and brought the binoculars back to her eyes and checked again for movement, for cars, for trucks. For tanks and soldiers.

The shallow valley their informant had sent them to had struck her right away as an alien landscape. Though perhaps a year had passed, you could still find the marks of backhoes and graders, and the grass was lush and new, no animal paths in the expanse; it looked like a lawn that had been seeded, a think carpet of green the Serbs thought hid what they'd done here. Alexei had been careful to strip the sod away before he dug, so he could replace it with no one's being the wiser that they'd been here. The Serbs had been known to dig up a mass grave and move the bones somewhere else if they thought the location had become known.

She stowed the binoculars in the pack on her back and used her eyes to sweep, to spot a glint of light that could mean anything from a stray shard of glass to the scope of a sniper rifle. Nothing. Trees, a few cattle a dozen hills away, rocks, and this valley of grass where all the others were stone and scrub.

"Mai?"

Alexei hadn't shouted but had allowed for the "bowl" of the valley to carry his voice up to her. She turned to see his blue-gloved hands holding a skull up over his head, the most obscene present he'd ever given her.

She scooted back down the hill and stood at the edge of the small trench Alexei had dug. On the floor of the trench she saw the rounded humps of more skulls, the stripes of ribs, almost invisible because they'd absorbed the color of the surrounding dirt.

Mai took in the relatively small size of Alexei's dig and the size of the flat-bottomed hollow and extrapolated they stood on a mass grave for several hundred Bosnian Muslims. She took her camera from her pack and began to take pictures. Alexei had placed the skull on the edge of the tarp, and it stared at her, its eyeless sockets asking her to show this to the world.

Alexei brought out a GPS unit and saved the coordinates of the location. The two of them worked the rest of the day refilling the hole, tamping the dirt down with their boots, and re-laying the sod after carrying multiple canteens of water from the small stream nearby so the grass wouldn't die and betray their intrusion. Almost with reverence, Alexei had wrapped the skull in gauze from their first-aid kit before he stowed it in an evidence bag. As they hiked from the site back to their vehicle hidden in a cave, Mai couldn't stop staring at Alexei's backpack, where the skull rode. She could still see the skull's eyes begging her.

After he tried the door to the hotel suite's bedroom and found it locked, Alexei Bukharin tapped on it. When there was no answer, he knocked harder.

"What the fuck is this?" he muttered and glanced around the living area of the suite. Yes, the desk was the logical place. He rummaged through the drawers, found the universal key for any of the doors inside the suite, and stalked back to the bedroom door and opened it.

Mai's clothes from their trek lay tossed about on the floor. Her gun belt and gun lay on the bed, but Mai was no where to be seen. He heard a soft splash of water and looked in the bathroom.

Mai lay in the full tub, steam rising and bubbles popping, her head on a vinyl pillow. Her eyes were closed. Her left arm was outside the tub, dangling over the side, and her hand clutched the neck of a bottle of Jameson. A good third of its contents were gone, likely sloshing inside her stomach hidden below the froth of bubbles. He watched as she brought the bottle to her mouth and drank without opening her eyes.

"I know you're there," she said.

"I didn't exactly use stealth," Alexei replied. He walked to the tub, sat on the floor beside it, and took the bottle from her fingers. He took a drink, winced, and put it back in her hand. "Why was the door locked?" he asked her.

"Because I wanted privacy, which, as usual, you took upon yourself to disrupt."

"If you'd said, 'Alexei, I want some privacy,' I wouldn't be here."

She opened her eyes, fixed her stare on him, and said, "Alexei, I want some privacy."

"Sorry, too late."

"Yes, my point exactly. What do you want?"

"To know why you locked the door."

"Did I need to speak Russian?" she asked.

"Mai, I understand you're angry at what we found. I'm angry, too, but I didn't put those men in the ground."

"Surely you've known me long enough to understand it's because you're convenient?"

"Yes, I think I figured that out." He traced a finger down her bare arm and stared at the line of bubbles that showed the swell of her breasts and the hint of something more. "I agree that a good dose of liquor will let us sleep deep enough there'll be no dreams, but let me order some room service so we don't pull a drunk on empty stomachs."

"Well, this is a first, certainly."

"What is?"

"You're thinking about eating and not sex."

Alexei smiled and let his finger brush her arm again. "Actually, I'm waiting for more bubbles to dissolve so I can see your nipples, but I'm more hungry right now than horny."

That got a brief smirk from her. "Something light for me," she said, "since I've had a good start on the whiskey. I'll join you in the other room in a few minutes."

"Wearing only bubbles?"

The laugh was as fleeting as the smile. She muttered, "Get on with you, then," and handed him the bottle of whiskey as she reached for a towel.

In her whiskey-clouded dreams, she walked through a valley with the shadow of death, bony hands thrusting through the soil and grass to clutch at her. Mute voices from hundreds of skulls cried out, and she heard. And she didn't fear the evil that had come here and left death behind. Truth always overcame evil, and she did not want for truth.

- 22 -

ANGEL OF DEATH

Bosnia-Herzegovina, 2000

" A t the crossroads, turn right, and you'll see the castle," her
informant had said.

Mai Fisher had been dubious, not of the accuracy of the
directions but of the informant himself. It wouldn't be the first time in
Serbia she'd paid for information only to be sent in the wrong direction; it
wouldn't be the last.

She drove along the country road, her lights off, relying on her instincts
and the approaching dawn to show her the way. She reached the crossroads
and made the right turn onto a narrower track. To her shock, the informant
hadn't led her wrong. The castle was there, clinging to the side of a
mountain overlooking the Danube, but it was there.

She angled her vehicle off the road and into some brush that would give
it camouflage. After checking she had plenty of ammo for her Beretta and a
flashlight in her vest, she left the vehicle. Keeping to the tree-line, she made
her way to the foot of a long set of stairs that led to this rear tower of the
castle. She saw it had at least a half-dozen different sets of stairs leading
from it, some going up and over the hill, some down toward the water, and
the set she was about to climb, which was shielded from view by an
outcropping of rock. It led to the lowest-level entrance to the tower, also
hidden from easy view.

The tower had probably served as a storage area when the castle was
occupied, or perhaps had been an escape route in the unlikely event
someone had overrun the main castle. That had recently been restored as a
popular tourist spot, but this two- or three-story tower was closed off from

the main area and gave Mai the impression it could fall into Danube below at any moment.

Her booted feet silent on the stairs, Mai began her climb to the arched entrance. The doorway was ink-black against the gray stone, and her brain took that moment to dredge up a memory of some Indiana Jones movie where the walls and floor of an ancient structure crawled with a layer of beetles. That started a trickle of sweat down her back, and when she stood before the archway with its locked, wrought-iron grate, she dared to use the flashlight to check the immediate area. Bug-free, it seemed, and she hoped the cold air would keep them dormant.

Now to see if the rest of what she'd bought from the informant was true. A smaller, dark square in the stone above and to the left of the arch was where the informant said the key to the grate's padlock would be. She tipped up on her toes and groped for the recess only to mutter a curse of frustration when she realized it was just out of her reach. Her eyes searched the area around the archway, and she saw a rock had tumbled down the hill, some time ago given the amount of moss covering it. A good foot high, it should give her enough of a boost to reach the key.

She spent an awkward moment balanced on one foot on the rock, but her gloved hand closed around the key, and she hopped down. The padlock itself was an old one, large and heavy, its patina making it ominous. Dead center of the lock was the over-sized keyhole, and the key itself was large and ornate and as old. Mai wondered if it would operate at all, if this was another wild goose chase in pursuit of justice.

When she turned the key, the lock operated smoothly, though the "click" was louder than she wanted, and the shank opened easily. An old lock in good operating condition. Someone wanted to make certain access to this tower was easy. That was confirmed when she opened the grate and it didn't make a noise. Not a groan or a creak. She glanced back over her shoulder. You could move any amount of contraband in and out of this entrance and never worry about being seen. Maybe the information she'd purchased was good after all.

Mai peered inside the tower before she stepped in and could see about ten feet. After that, she'd be in darkness. The Beretta came out, an extension of her hand, and she attached the noise suppressor. She couldn't risk the flashlight, and took a deep breath before she entered the tunnel, gun held up before her.

After a few feet, she could see a soft glow. She'd seen no light leaking from any of the tower's windows, so the stairs must lead to an interior room. She kept her progress slow to let her eyes adjust gradually, and she slowed even more as she crept up the interior stairs.

She emerged into a hallway and slipped quickly to her right, going up a few steps of the stairway that led to the upper levels. The glance had been brief, but she'd seen two men—one, large and flabby, seated at a table; the other, lean and buff, standing across the table from the first.

"You should have told me you didn't have cash," said one man. She wasn't sure which, but his Serbian was native.

"You've taken this credit card before," said the other. Definitely an American by his accent when he spoke Serbian.

"Cash next time," said the first man. "Or your privileges get cut off." Mai heard the distinct sound of a manual credit card slide being operated.

"Get some fresh stuff in here," the American said. "These are getting too used."

"Two weeks, and I'll have a new shipment. Very fresh. Very new," the Serb said in English. "Bring cash."

"Cash it is. Later, Lazar."

Mai pressed herself against the wall of the stairwell as the American walked past. She was able to see the logo on the upper sleeve of his jacket—a red rectangle with three white, block letters denoting a U.S. engineering company, which had built Camp Bondsteel for U.S. troops in Kosova. He didn't go down the steps she'd climbed but took a short hallway to his right and disappeared down another flight of stairs.

She waited until she heard his footsteps fade and the faint sound of a car starting before she crept down the steps and peered into the anteroom beyond.

The large Serb sat at his table, his back mostly to her as he counted money and wrote in a notebook. On the wall behind him were two rows of six hooks, each holding a numbered, green tag with a key. One key tag was missing. On a carabineer hooked to a belt loop on Lazar's pants was a key similar to the one she'd used on the grate. He had a Ruger P90 jammed in his waist band at the small of his back.

Mai heard a soft sound. Weeping. Muffled but nearby, a child was crying.

Lazar's head came up as he paused in his bookwork. "Shut up, you little cunts!" he shouted. The crying intensified, joined by others. "That's it. No breakfast for you little whores!"

Mai stepped into the light, gun up in both hands. "Lazar," she said.

He jerked around, stunned he wasn't alone. She gave him a moment to recognize her, and she put two rounds into his chest. Lazar tipped backward in his chair, his head cracking against the stone wall, and he was still. Keeping the gun on him, she went to the table and flipped the pages of the notebook. She smiled as she picked it up and tucked it inside her vest. His client list.

The money she left, but she took the credit card receipt for the American's card and noted his name. She noted as well it was a U.S. Defense Department credit card, issued to one of its contractors.

She went to Lazar, stepped over the pool of blood, and unclipped the key from his belt loop. A footfall made her flatten herself against the wall and aim her gun toward the sound, but she lowered it.

Wearing a thin, knee-length shift, a girl stood there. Her hair, though now mussed, had been done up in an adult way, as had the makeup, which had run. Streaks of black mascara scored her cheeks, and the red lipstick had been smudged in a circle around her swollen lips. She clutched a key tag in her small fist, and when she'd seen Mai's gun, her bladder let go.

"Don't worry," Mai said in Serbian. "It's all right. I won't hurt you."

The girl's world-weary eyes settled on Lazar. "Is he dead?" she asked.

"Yes," Mai said. "I'm here to take you someplace safe."

The unsettling eyes focused on Mai. "Are you her? The one they used to talk about, *Smrt Anjleo*?"

"That's a myth," Mai said. "How many of you are there?"

"Twelve. Why couldn't you have come last week?"

Mai frowned and shook her head. "What?"

"My sister. They took her away last week because she was pregnant and beginning to show. Why couldn't you have come then?"

Mai felt her throat close off her words. It had been the body of a young, pregnant girl washed up on a Danube shore that had led her to look into the rumors of what went on here.

"I'm sorry," Mai said. "I didn't know about this place until now. What is your name?"

"What is yours?"

Mai smiled at the child's spirit. "I'm Maiya," she said, using her Russian nickname. "How old are you?"

"I am Zora, and I am fifteen years old. My sister was Dragana, and she was thirteen. Will you help me find her?"

The inability to speak overcame Mai again and made her push her feelings away. "I will help you, but let's get the others out of here first. I have a vehicle, and I'll take you to a safe place where no one else will hurt you. I promise."

"I will only believe the word of *Smrt Anjleo*."

"And you have it," Mai said.

Zora walked to the rows of keys and replaced the missing one. She took Mai by the hand and led her down a hallway to a door. Mai saw it was steel-reinforced and recently installed.

"We all stay here," Zora said. "When a man comes with a room key, he picks one of us, and we go upstairs and fuck."

The anger that rose in Mai almost made her go back and kill Lazar all over again, but she showed only a calm face as she unlocked the door. Before she could open it, Zora lay a hand on her arm.

"Inside, the smell is very bad," she said. "We call this room *pakao*."

When Mai opened the door, she saw, indeed, some level of hell.

Neil Boyler slid his money through the slot at the bottom of the panel of bullet-proof glass. The old man behind it counted the money before he put the room key through the slot. Boyler took the key but leaned down to the grille in the glass.

"She's a virgin, right? A young virgin?" he asked.

The old man gave a very Serbian shrug. "You paid your money," he said. "You'll get what you paid for."

"If I don't, I'll be back with a bulldozer and bury you under this building."

Boyler had been irked when Lazar had gone missing. Lazar had a knack for finding what Boyler needed—girls, the younger the better. A friend of Lazar's had recommended this place, and none too soon. Boyler was aching for a cherry to pop.

By the time he reached the second floor and found the room, he was more than ready for what was waiting for him. He pictured it in his head—thirteen or fourteen, blonde hair, pretty blue eyes, breasts just budding. When he opened the door, he was licking his lips.

The room was nothing special—a bed with clean sheets and a bathroom with running water. He wasn't alarmed when he saw no one in the room. Sometimes the girls tried to hide, and finding them and pulling them by their hair from the hiding place was the best turn-on.

"Don't hide, sweetie," he said in Serbian. "I've got candy here. Nice chocolate for you. Come on out and let me see you."

He was so hard now it was almost painful, and that meant he'd hurt the little bitch and make it all the better.

Boyler heard a throat-clearing behind him and turned, smile on his face. A woman, a full-grown woman, stood in the doorway, and he seethed at the thought the old man downstairs had fucked him over.

"What's the matter, Neil?" the woman asked, her British accent incongruous in a Belgrade hotel that had seen better days a generation ago. "Am I too old for you?"

Boyler felt his erection wilt as a line of sweat popped on his upper lip. "I don't know what you're talking about," he said. "Who are you?"

"Oh," she said, with a faint smile, "the person who put two bullets in a pimp named Lazar."

"Who? I've never heard of anyone…"

"I have your credit card receipt," she said. "I have Lazar's ledger. He kept excellent records, no doubt for a little blackmail down the road. Names, dates, which girl. Your wife back in Sioux Falls has a copy."

Boyler lunged forward to push the woman from between him and the door, but she was faster. A knee to his stomach, an elbow between his shoulder blades, and he was on the floor gasping for breath. The woman grabbed him by his collar and dragged him to the bed. She pulled his left arm over his head, and he felt something hard and cold clamp down on his wrist. He twisted his head to see as she closed the other half of the handcuffs on the metal bedpost.

"Oh, God," he said, "oh, God, please, please, please, don't kill me! Please don't kill me!"

The woman pressed her gloved hand over his mouth. "I'll wager those girls, those little girls, begged you not to hurt them, didn't they?" she said. Tears clouded Boyler's eyes, and he was glad not to see the woman's face. It was like soldiers he'd seen at the base, the special operations guys, the ones with the 1,000-mile stare. "It made you hard, didn't it?" she asked. Her hand moved and clutched his throat. "Answer me. It made you hard, didn't it?"

"Yes," he grunted. "Please, don't kill me. Please. I have children."

She leaned down, her face inches from his. "I know you do. Two daughters. Your wife is having a doctor examine them to see if you've raped them, too."

"I never, I never..."

"Oh, I see, it has to be somebody else's little girls, does it?" Her hand clenched tighter. "Answer me."

"Yes, yes!"

She released his throat and seated herself in a rickety chair next to the bed. When Boyler looked at her, she was still smiling, and he almost vomited on himself.

"What shall I do with you, Neil?" she asked. "I could take you to the Serbian police, but, frankly, their record on human trafficking is appalling, and, well, some of the names in Lazar's ledger were highly placed policemen. Let's see. The U.S. Army? No, not their jurisdiction. The only thing they'd do is have your employer ship you home, and letting you off unscathed doesn't sit well with me. No, I think a more personal touch is what you need."

His heart beating a rapid tattoo within his chest, Boyler watched her cross the room and open the door. A man entered, his face bearing the weathered look of someone who worked outdoors. He could have been thirty or forty, but there was no way to tell. His hands and forearms were knotted with muscles, and though he was barely taller than the woman, Boyler thought the man would be the winner in any brawl he had.

"Neil," the woman said, "this is Zoran Grujic. He's a farmer, and he had two daughters. One of them, Lazar killed when her pregnancy began to show. The older one, Zora, was the last girl you raped before I put Lazar out of his miserable existence."

"Who? I don't know what…"

"Of course, you'd never be bothered to learn the names." She looked from Neil to the other man, whose eyes bored into him. "Well, then, I'll leave you two to talk."

The woman walked toward the door. "No, wait!" Boyler shouted. "You can't leave me here with this guy! You can't, for the love of God!"

She turned back, that smile on her face again. "Sorry, Neil, I don't believe in God, but I do believe in justice."

The man named Zoran nodded to her, not a nod actually. More of a bow, and the woman left the room, shutting the door behind her.

The two men stared at each other again, Boyler's breath coming in gasps, his heart beating so fast and hard, he couldn't speak. He watched as Zoran removed his jacket, folded it neatly, and lay it aside. Zoran walked to the bedside table and turned on the old radio there. He cranked the volume as loud as it would go, and Boyler screamed.

Author's note: Smrt Anjleo *loosely translates from the Serbian as "Death Angel," or Angel of Death.*

- 23 -

PEP TALK

Directorate Training Facility, 2004

Zora Doxie led her two team members through the dark toward the house. At the hedge surrounding the yard, she knelt, her clenched fist upraised. Kelley Wooton settled beside her on the left, Tyrone Cape on the right.

"Check it with the goggles, Ty," she whispered.

"No heat signatures," he said. "We're good."

She motioned the other two to spread out, and, low to the ground, the three of them crept across the back lawn to the dark and silent house. As she approached the door, Zora considered what approach to take.

A dynamic entry—Ty loved kicking in doors—or a quieter break-in? Sure, they were out in the middle of nowhere, but discretion was the best bet.

As the two men stood nearby, their eyes and weapons scanning their surroundings, Zora slipped a credit card from her pocket and used it to force the simple door knob lock. Her night vision goggles over her eyes, rifle tucked against her shoulder, she counted down with her fingers—three, two, one.

Zora pushed the door open and entered, the two men behind her moving inside and to her right and left again.

Their boots quiet on the carpeted floor, they cleared each room, meeting up in the office.

"Time check," she said.

"We got twelve minutes left," Ty said.

"Get working on the safe, Kel," Zora said.

Wooton knelt before the desk-sized safe and took out his stethoscope. Zora went to the window that looked out onto the front of the house and checked for any interlopers, the seconds counting off in her head.

"Got it," she heard Wooton say.

"Check for booby traps," Zora told him.

"Come on, Zo Dee. You think I'm just outta basic. Watch your eyes."

They all raised their goggles as Wooton used a small flashlight to check for wires or other obvious booby traps. He was apparently satisfied because he eased the safe door open. The beam from his flashlight landed on a metal strongbox.

"Well, shit," Wooton muttered. "This is a different kind of lock. It's going to take me a while."

"Well, take the strongbox," Tyrone said.

"Good idea, Ty," Zora said. "Take it, Kel."

Wooton took the time to check for a pressure plate or tripwires or both and lifted the strongbox from the safe with care.

"Whoa, pretty heavy," he said.

"You got it?" Zora asked.

"Yeah, I'm good."

"All right, let's go."

With Zora leading the way, they retraced their route through the house. She peered through the window in the door, saw nothing and no one, and led the way into the back yard.

Wooton was the first to go down, hit in the knee and the neck. The strongbox he'd carried dropped from his hands to land with a thunk on the hard ground. Ty fell next, two to the chest. Zora brought her rifle up. Too late. She took two in the chest as well.

"Lights!" someone shouted, and the back yard lit up under the glare of high-power spotlights.

Zora stared up at a black-clad figure with only its eyes visible, looking for all the world like an alien. Zora raised up on her elbows and looked down at the smears of blue paint on her tactical vest. The figure looming over them reached up and pulled off a balaclava. Zora almost cringed but felt her anger flare. It would be this instructor.

"Well," Mai Fisher said, "this was a cluster-fuck."

"Begging the instructor's pardon," Wooton said, and coughed. "But we got the box. We attained the objective."

"That may be the case, Mr. Wooton," Fisher said, "but you didn't get it back to base, and if I'd used bullets instead of paint balls, you'd be dead. So you didn't 'attain the objective.' All right, I'll see you all in the morning at the debriefing, where I will point out in excruciating detail exactly where you got it wrong. Have a nice evening."

The three got to their feet. "Bitch," Tyrone muttered.

"Thank you, Mr. Cape," Fisher's voice trailed back to them.

"Ty, man, don't make it worse," Wooton said.

Zora thought it unlikely to get any worse than this.

Mai sat with the other instructors, reviewing the video of the training session from the night before. The lead instructor, Max Torpey, shook his head.

"Doxie should have known better," he said.

"Yeah, she was too focused on beating the time limit," said Fernando Cacho.

Torpey looked over at Mai. "She sees herself in a competition with you," he said to her.

"Me?" Mai replied. "I'm out of field work. Why would she think that?"

"Well, Chica, you got a rep," Cacho said. "All the female recruits want to better your times."

"And I'm sure none of you encourage that," Mai said.

"Doxie's got potential," Torpey said.

"She does," Mai replied, "but she needs to focus."

"Go explain to her the competition is all in her head," Torpey said.

He and Cacho left her alone to watch the video again. Halfway through, she stopped it, picked up her coffee, and headed for the debriefing room. When she opened the door and stepped in, she saw Doxie, Wooton, and Cape huddled together, their heads almost touching. She caught Wooton with his mouth open, and she saw Doxie was dressed all in black, her dark hair, with its prominent widow's peak, French-braided.

Dear God, Mai thought, as she stood there, dressed in black and with her hair in a French braid. "Good morning," she said as she took a seat across from them. They shifted away from each other, so their chairs were evenly spaced apart.

They each muttered some version of "good morning" in return and gave her neutral expressions.

"So, rather than my stating the obvious, why don't you outline for me what went wrong?" Mai told them.

The three exchanged glances, and Mai saw the warning look Cape gave Doxie. Mai wondered how deep that relationship was.

Zora Doxie leveled a steely stare on Mai and said, "You cheated."

Mai saw Wooton hang his head, and Cape rolled his eyes. Their discussion before Mai's arrival must have been about what to say to Mai, and the two men had lost the argument.

"What makes you say that?" Mai asked.

"Your participation was not included in the action planning," Doxie said.

"I wasn't aware covert ops functioned on a specific agenda," Mai replied. "Unexpected things pop up, you have to deal with them, but I'm more interested in specifics not speculation."

"We shoulda left someone on the back door," Wooton said. "Night vision goggles would have spotted you."

"Three people clearing the house took less time," Doxie said.

"Time wasn't a parameter," Mai said.

"We were told, and I quote, 'The time to beat is fifteen minutes,'" Doxie replied.

"That was motivation, not a requirement."

"Why introduce it?" Doxie asked.

Mai sipped her coffee, her eyes locked with Doxie's. She lowered the cup and said, "Gentlemen, give us the room."

"Ma'am?" Cape said.

"Don't ma'am me, and what exactly wasn't I clear about?" Mai said, her eyes never leaving Doxie.

When the two women were alone, Mai set her cup aside and leaned back in the chair. "What's your issue, Doxie?" she asked.

"None, Ms. Fisher."

"Interesting choice of wardrobe and hairstyle. Am I supposed to be flattered?"

Doxie flushed at that, her eyes breaking contact for a second before she recovered herself. "Coincidence," she said.

"You and I," Mai said, "are not in competition. I'm retired from field work. I'm simply here to teach and assess."

"You may not think it's a competition, but it is. You're into everything. The other instructors hold you up as some sort of holy icon the rest of us are supposed to worship."

"And the word on you is you're a Mossad reject."

Doxie stiffened and leaned forward, a finger pointed at Mai. "That is not true. I never applied to Mossad. Your Tel Aviv satellite office recruited me."

"And you thought you'd come here and be a star, have it all handed to you?"

"Of course not."

"Stop acting like you can't make a mistake. You rolled the dice on that training op last night and came up snake eyes." Mai saw the Israeli frown until she worked out the idiom. "Do you think that never happened to me?"

"You're the perfect op. That's what we hear all the time."

"Not when I'm around," Mai said. "I'm far from perfect, and I have the scars to show for it. However, I always made certain there'd be no complaints about my work."

Mai almost sighed aloud. Pep talks weren't her forte, and she suspected she'd end up making Doxie's attitude worse.

"I don't want you to be me," Mai continued. "What I want is for you to be a good operative so that we don't have to send you back to Tel Aviv in a box covered in a U.N. flag. You probably aren't interested in hearing this, but you're a captive audience and maybe I'll get through the wall you're building around yourself."

"What wa..."

"No, I'm talking now. You're listening. I'll let you know when you can speak. Thirty years ago when I was recruited, the prevailing sentiment was that I could fill and clear dead drops, pass along gossip from society parties. That or, once I 'matured,' I could be used as a swallow to seduce men or women into giving up their secrets or to compromise them. I decided I wouldn't conform to the stereotype.

"Being in operations meant that everything I did, every decision I made, was scrutinized far more deeply than my partner's. I took shite and more so the women who came after me wouldn't have to go through the same. If you want to see that as competition, frankly, Zora Doxie, Israeli Army hero, you have no business here. It will pain me, briefly only, I assure you, to go tell the assessment panel you don't have what it takes, but I'll do it. No qualms. By next week, I won't even remember your name."

Mai picked up her cup again and drank, studying the emotions playing over Doxie's face.

"Permission to speak freely?" Doxie asked.

"This isn't the military, but go ahead."

"You may not see it as a competition, but the other instructors gauge women recruits against your standard and take great pleasure in telling us how far short we fall."

"I'll have a word with them to put a stop to that. Using me to measure against is not my intention, and don't you understand, what they're hoping for is that we'll go at each other for their amusement?"

"What do you mean?"

"This may be 2004, Zora, but men are men. The instructors would find it stimulating if we were to fight each other."

"What? You mean, like, hand to hand?"

"Oh, yes, and if it were outside in the mud on a rainy day, they'd probably burst a vein with excitement."

"You're serious, aren't you?" Doxie asked.

"Yes, I am. I've been at this a long time. Some things don't change. Now, take some advice—or don't. It's up to you. Stop second guessing yourself, stop comparing yourself to me. That's a losing game because my husband tells me I'm incomparable." Mai gave her a smile that wasn't returned. Apparently, Zora Doxie was a hard-ass from the get-go. Mai had

had to work into it. "Forget I exist and be who you are," Mai continued. "Choose what you want to be. Don't let anyone else, least of all a warped image of me, dictate to you what you'll be."

"Is that what you did?"

"Yes, but the difference is I had to fight for it, fight hard. You don't. The Directorate can be the best place on earth to work or the most miserable, but that's up to you. So, ditch the black outfits—that's my signature, by the way, and I'm not flattered—and let your hair down or cut it or put it up in a ponytail, but don't try to be me."

"Because I need to be myself?"

"Because you'd fail. I'm incomparable, remember."

Mai saw the resentment, but she also saw Doxie tamp it down and thought perhaps she'd made a point after all.

After a moment Doxie said, "Do you miss it? Field work?"

"Why do you think I inserted myself in your training op? Of course I miss it, but this--" She waved a hand in the vague direction of the training hall. "--is what I do now. And I'm as hard-ass about this as I was about a mission. My mission now, Ms. Doxie, is to turn chunks of carbon like you into shiny, hard diamonds who go out and get the job done for The Directorate. I take that very seriously."

"That much is obvious."

"Good, because I've about run out of clichés to employ." That got a hint of a smile from Doxie. "One more question. What's between you and Tyrone Cape?" Mai asked.

Doxie blushed but didn't break eye contact. "Is that pertinent?"

"Probably not, but answer me."

"Well, you've seen him," Doxie said, this time with a smile as if between best friends. "He is a chick magnet, I believe the Americans say."

"Indeed. I married one of those. It took far too many years to reverse his polarity in that regard. Another piece of advice. You shouldn't make that attraction obvious in case you ever work together. I picked up on it too easily, and if I were your enemy, I'd exploit that any way I could." And she planned on doing that at the next training opportunity. "Any questions?" Mai asked.

"Do you know Krav Maga?" Doxie asked.

Mai smiled as a fond memory emerged. "Yes. Yoni Netanyahu taught me not long before he died."

"You must have been very young."

"I was eighteen and had a little crush on him, but, then, he was a 'chick-magnet,' too. Why do you ask?"

Doxie's smile was now conspiratorial. "I thought perhaps we could stage a little demonstration, perhaps set up a pool for who would win, and deprive the gentlemen of their hard-earned cash," she said.

Mai laughed and said, "I like the way you think, Zora Doxie."

"I have an excellent role model."

- 24 -

CLOSURE

Abbottabad, Pakistan, 2011

Mai hadn't had the falling dream for a long time. A decade at least. She suspected why it had returned, but the passage of time allowed her to control her reaction. Alexei's hand tightened a bit where it rested on her hip, but he didn't wake. Before, when the dreams came, she would wake anyone within earshot with her screaming.

In the dreams she didn't succeed in climbing from a makeshift tomb created by the collapse of Number Two World Trade Center; as she reached the break in the debris field that would lead to freedom, her foot would slip, and she began the six-story plummet. At least she woke before she hit.

Mai slipped from bed without waking Alexei and wrapped one of the extra blankets around her shoulders. After that particular dream, she could never stand being indoors.

She stood on the balcony before she remembered her hair was uncovered. Fuck it. It was the middle of the night. Who cared if anyone could see her hair?

Out of habit she checked the courtyard of the rented house. The non-functioning water fountain shined white in the moonlight, and a slight breeze stirred the clothing hung out this afternoon by the woman who helped with their housework. A widow with five, young children, she was grateful for the kind of work that didn't compromise her virtue. Cooking and cleaning for a "nice British couple" her family approved of, since she'd work mostly with Mai. This was an arrangement common in this upper, middle class neighborhood of Abbottabad, Pakistan. The woman was a font of information as well, gossiping about the comings and goings in the neighborhood.

Wealthy Pakistanis came here for the temperate climate, and tourists found it pleasing also. Many structures and parts of the surrounding hillsides still bore the scars from the massive earthquake a few years back. Landslides had gouged chunks from the hills, and, since nothing had grown back to disguise the wounded earth, Mai thought it looked as if some alien spaceship had descended and carved away pieces of the landscape. Surrounded by tree-covered mountains that offered otherwise spectacular scenery, secure because of the main Pakistani military academy not far away, and well away from the dirty, crowded principal cities like Karachi or Peshawar, Abbottabad was a polished gem in a country disrupted by military coups, poverty, and corruption.

Shaped like an L and surrounded by an eight-foot stone wall, the two-story house she'd called home for the past few weeks was similar in some respects to the one down the street, the one they were here to watch. In reflex, Mai picked up the night vision binoculars from a table on the balcony and focused them on the compound three blocks away.

She wasn't the only one who couldn't sleep.

A tall, bearded man in a light-colored *shalwar*, his head covered with a plain *taqiyah* or skullcap, paced back and forth on a small balcony. Hands clasped behind his back, his eyes cast down, he seemed deep in thought as he paced.

What thoughts, she wondered, bounced around inside that head?

If she had a sniper rifle, this would all be over in a few seconds, and she and Alexei could go back into retirement.

At least she hadn't been the one to bring them back into the field. This time. No, Alexei had volunteered their services, but after two months here all they'd had were glimpses, like this one, of a man whose identity they were certain of but couldn't yet prove.

Short of walking up to the guarded gate in that compound and ringing the bell, she still wasn't sure how they'd go about proving his identity. The CIA was getting antsy and impatient, and Alexei had promised they'd deliver. After gifting the CIA with hundreds of photos of the compound and the people coming and going from it, but without the money shot, even Mai was almost ready to pack it in.

She understood, she really did, the need for caution, the need to be absolutely certain this man was their target. It made no difference she and Alexei were 100% confident of his identity; with this mission it had to be beyond question. Given their history with the man, they could, quite rightly, be accused of bias.

Alexei had wanted to call on his KGB roots and kidnap one of the women in the compound. Every four days, clad in a burqa, a woman left with a guard and went to the local market. Their target had married and divorced several wives and tended to marry to cement alliances, Mai had argued. If they kidnapped one wife, the target would flee, divorce that one, and marry another.

Mai had opted for bribery and seduction, using a variety of stringers for both. The guards had proved un-bribable and incapable of being seduced. Whether that was from loyalty to their leader or religious conviction, she didn't know, but it had frustrated her that time-proven techniques had failed.

She longed again for the sniper rifle, but that sort of revenge should belong to Alexei. His list of grievances was longer—a dead brother from the Soviet-Afghan War and a dead wife from September 11—or so he'd thought for months. She supposed seeing a 110-story building, one your wife was in, collapse would be reason enough to assume she was dead. He'd forgotten, however, how stubborn she was about not dying. It was a bone of contention, even a decade later, she occasionally dug up, that he could assume widower status with such swift ease.

That was in the past, and they were here, now, with long-desired closure at hand.

"Bad dream?"

She heard the question from behind her and nodded. She turned to Alexei, setting the binoculars aside.

"Did I wake you?" she asked.

"No, that was my sixty-seven-year-old prostate," he said.

He stood in the doorway, his white hair lit by the moonlight. His beard was neatly clipped, unlike the one he'd sported a decade ago when he'd hunted this same quarry in Afghanistan.

"See anything?" he asked.

"He can't sleep either."

"Somehow I doubt he has bad dreams or has his sleep disturbed by conscience," Alexei said. He didn't pick up the binoculars but squinted in the direction of the compound. "A sniper rifle would be nice."

"I was thinking that."

"Tired of our vacation spot so soon?" he asked, and she saw him smile.

"Two months is a long 'vacation.' Short of sending his head to the CIA in a box, I don't know how we're going to prove to them it's he."

"We only need a small sample of his DNA," Alexei said.

"They burn their trash in the compound, so there's no way we can trash-pick, as delightful a prospect as that is. He never leaves there, we can't get inside…"

"Maybe we can't but perhaps there's someone who can."

Mai stepped back inside and slid the door to the balcony closed—in case they weren't the only ones with a parabolic microphone.

"What do you mean?" she asked.

"The government doctor who lives a few doors down? He's been in the compound before when one of the women had a 'female issue.' His words. He talks a lot about Islam and how al Qaeda have perverted it."

"You're going to recruit him?"

"I'm close. I hadn't said anything before now because I wasn't sure enough of him, but he's ready to come over."

"You know very well if our subject has a medical problem, he wouldn't call on an unknown, provincial doctor," Mai said.

"True, he'd go to a military hospital like he did the last time. There was an item in the Karachi newspaper, which the doctor pointed out to me. A measles outbreak not far from here. He expects the government to require vaccinations."

He wasn't being obtuse. She knew that. Rather, he knew she'd put it together, and she did. "We'd have to mark a syringe," she said, "so we don't have to test several thousand."

"And I'm sure the doctor will need a nurse for when he vaccinates the women," Alexei said, a smile again quirking his mouth.

She pointed a finger at him as she headed back to the bed. "I'll do anything," she told him, "to have that beard gone."

The tall, dark-skinned man, his suit immaculate, strode from a side door to a lectern flanked by American flags. He set his serious gaze on the camera before him and began to speak.

"Good evening. Tonight, I can report to the American people and to the world that the United States has conducted an operation that killed Osama bin Laden, the leader of Al-Qaeda, and a terrorist who's responsible for the murder of thousands of innocent men, women, and children."

- 25 -

26 MAY 2011

Former Republic of Yugoslavia, 2011

"Well, I must say, the two of you have not aged, that I can see," said Vojislav Ranovesic.

Alexei Bukharin shook hands with Ranovesic. "Looks are deceiving," Alexei said, with a smile. "There are advantages and disadvantages on the approach to seventy years of age."

"If he starts complaining about his prostate," Mai Fisher said, though with a wink at her husband, "ignore him. You're looking well, too, Voja. And you've changed jobs, I see."

"Yes, the two of you were a bad influence that year in Belgrade. I switched from the federal police to the Security Information Agency," the former Serb policeman said. The SIA was Serbia's intelligence organization, a much different job from what he'd had as a police captain. Ranovesic looked them over again and smiled. "And you're here as…"

"Representatives of the War Crimes Prosecutor's Office," Mai replied.

"Ah, yes, of course." Ranovesic nodded, though some skepticism showed on his face.

"Does it matter whom we represent?" Alexei asked. "Each of us has the same interest in justice."

"Indeed we do, and for this one, what is it Americans would say? We have hit ball from park." The policeman—Mai and Alexei would always think of him that way—motioned like a baseball player and grinned with undisguised glee. "But this operation belongs to the special police," he added. "I'm merely along to gather intelligence."

137

"And we're here for a third-party confirmation that this is Ratko Mladic," Mai said. "We have a medical technician with us, with the equipment necessary to test DNA."

"What's the plan?" Alexei asked, focused on the action, as always.

"And I thought you retired?" Ranovesic asked, giving Mai a smile.

"I did, and you'll notice I'll be letting the youngsters do the hard work. However," Alexei said, with a glance at his wife, "there is something to be said for closure. I saw what this bastard did at Srebrenica. His arrest will be like a retirement gift for me. The plan?"

"Two dozen special police. In Larazevo, they'll hit the houses of four of Mladic's relatives simultaneously. Mladic himself is living with his cousin Branislav. We've had him under surveillance for a couple of months. We're reasonably certain it's he, but..." Ranovesic broke off with a shrug. "After Mladic is secured, we go in, and you get to tell him he's going to The Hague."

"Then," Mai said, "let's do this."

For the most part, Alexei Bukharin dozed on the ride to the Banat region of northern Serbia. Theirs was a modest convoy—four special police Jeeps carrying black-clad policemen and the SIA bus, which was more like a mobile operations center, with Ranovesic's half-dozen men and the four-person War Crimes Prosecutor's team.

He brought himself awake and checked his watch. Not long until dawn, which meant they were close to their destination. The plan was to move on the four houses while the residents still slept. The Mladic clan was protective of their war criminal relative, and the element of surprise would lessen the likelihood of a firefight in a small Serbian town. Mladic had never been concerned about collateral damage, but Alexei knew Ranovesic was.

Alexei narrowed his eyes and stared Mai, who sat on the bench seat across from him. She didn't look like a woman in her early fifties. She was lean and fit and still ran a few miles every day. Her only vain indulgence was having her hair colored regularly so the gray wouldn't show. Most men would appreciate being with a woman who looked and acted twenty years younger than they, and he, in fact, did relish that. Rather, he had an acute awareness of their age difference, more so now than when she was nineteen and he was thirty-four, all those years ago. That, and she flatly refused to accept the fact that he was growing old.

Despite their recent assist for the CIA in the matter of Osama bin Laden, his retirement had finally settled into exactly that about five years ago. He still consulted with the War Crimes Tribunal, and Mai had replaced Nelson a few years before.

She turned to look at him, her incredibly dark eyes twinkling, a smile quirking her mouth. "I can hear you thinking," she said.

"Thinking about you," he replied.

"When did you become such a hopeless romantic?"

"Oh, about thirty-four years ago. It took me a while to realize it."

"I'm glad you did. And thank you for indulging me in this little escapade so soon after Abbottabad."

"It's my indulgence, too. I never lost my desire for justice. Rather, I doubted my continued effectiveness in achieving it."

"Milosevic and Tudjman dead, Karadizc arrested. Mladic in The Hague would lift a burden from the Serbian people," Mai said.

"Precisely why President Tadic is letting this arrest happen."

She nodded, her eyes drifting to stare at the dark outside the window. "We did good work here overall, didn't we?"

"Yes," he said. "I know there were times when that seemed in doubt, but after this morning is done, we can celebrate. Maybe I'll dance the *gopak*."

That got a laugh from her. "I remember I fell on my ass when you tried to teach me how to dance like a Cossack, but it would be worth it to see you do it again. I found it very sexy."

"I'd best work on strengthening my old knees." Alexei saw movement at the front of the bus and looked up as Ranovesic approached them.

"Ten minutes," Ranovesic said.

Alexei nodded, but Mai rose and picked up the small duffel she'd brought with her. Alexei watched as she stripped off her jacket, donned a ballistic vest, and strapped on her gun belt. She secured the tactical holster to her thigh. He hadn't seen her armed in quite a few years, and he was both aroused and dismayed by it. She caught his expression.

"Don't worry," she said, her smile assuring, "I'm not vaulting any fences with our secret police friends."

"But you'd like to," he said.

Her smile became a feral grin. "Oh, God, yes, but you're not the only one with old knees. I'll content myself with watching. Besides, you and I have all those years ahead of us still. I'm not taking any chances."

"I like your priorities."

Only the occasional dog or a boy kicking a soccer ball greeted the convoy that pulled up to four houses in the same block. Men in black masks and uniforms with no insignia struck all four houses like lightening. They didn't catch Mladic in bed, as they hoped, but they almost made the old man fall down the steps of his house as he set out to take an early morning walk.

Two policemen grabbed him and forced him to the floor with shouts and threats from their rifles. When his cousin, Branislav emerged in his robe to see what the noise was about, other policeman forced him against a wall.

Vojislav Ranovesic—Mai Fisher and Alexei Bukharin trailing behind him—strolled along the row of Serbian spruce trees that lined the Mladic lawn and entered the house. Somewhere a woman, perhaps Madame Mladic, wept, and the only other sound was the ragged breathing of the man face-down on the floor.

Ranovesic leaned down and grasped the man's collar, lifting his head slightly. He looked up at Mai and Alexei, a lifted eyebrow asking the question.

Alexei, the one who'd had most of the contact with the former Serbian general, nodded.

Ranovesic gave the man a shake. "Identify yourself!" he ordered. "Identify yourself now. Lie, and I will make it hard on you."

The voice was weaker now, no longer capable of bellowing at his troops after a series of strokes, but it was clear when he said, "General Ratko Mladic."

"Get him up off the floor," Ranovesic told the policemen. "Put him on the sofa."

They obeyed, and Mladic sat, slumped, looking nothing like the man who had ordered the deaths of 8,000-plus Bosnian Muslim men and boys at Srebrenica, who had laughed when one of his paramilitary commanders had ordered one man to eat the testicles of another on pain of death. The once-full face was thin, slack-skinned, though the eyes still were defiant. He looked up at the man and woman standing before him, and one side of his face smirked. The other didn't move.

"You," he said to them. "You take pleasure in scaring an old man nearly to death."

"I take pleasure only in justice," Mai said.

Mladic gave a snort of laughter. "Your Serbian is better."

"I've had practice."

Alexei turned to one of the policemen. "Go tell his wife to pack his medicines. Only that. Nothing more. Make certain of that. And don't give him the medications. We have a medical technician who'll check that they're really medicine. Give them to her."

The policeman nodded and went toward the bedroom.

The half-smirk came to Mladic's face again. "You think I'll kill myself?"

Mai said, "Milosevic did."

"I would be surprised if it weren't you who killed him in custody. Will you do the same for me, *kuchka*?"

"No, you won't get to skip your medication like Milosevic did. You'll live through your trial, Ratko. If we have to keep you alive with every machine possible, you'll be tried in court for your crimes."

"Get out of my sight."

"Not until I turn the key in the lock on your cell," Alexei said. "What a satisfying sound that will be. I think I'll film it for the widows and orphans of Srebrenica. I'll see every one of them gets a picture of you behind bars."

The old man sat back on the sofa and averted his gaze. Alexei turned and motioned the medical technician forward. General Ratko Mladic, the Butcher of Srebrenica, sat motionless as the technician took his blood pressure, checked his heart and lungs, and drew a blood sample. The police secured his wrists in cuffs and began to walk him toward the SIA bus. His legs faltered, and two of the policemen made a seat of their arms and carried him into the bus and into a room where a policeman would be with him until Mai and Alexei put him on a plane to The Hague.

The sun was fully up and people had gathered to watch. As the policemen milled about and kept the people away from the scene, Mai turned to Alexei.

"Where's my *gopak*?" she asked. When she saw the reluctance on his face, she gave him a fake pout. "You promised, and I'm sure I'll make it worth your while."

Alexei dropped into a squat, arms crossed over his chest, and kicked his right leg out then the left, a half-dozen or more times, enough to get the policeman clapping to the beat. Mai laughed with delight when he straightened, one arm in the air, other hand at his waist. He breathed a little hard, his face had a slight flush, but he said, "That was invigorating."

"The arrest or the *gopak*?" Mai asked, walking to his side and slipping an arm around his waist.

"Both, and I'm starving. Let's see what Ranovesic has to eat on that magnificent bus."

THE END

April 2012 - October 2012
Staunton, VA

ABOUT THE AUTHOR

P. A. Duncan is a retired bureaucrat but one with an overactive imagination—at least that's what everyone had told her since she first started making up stories in elementary school prompted by her weekly list of spelling words.

A commercial pilot and former FAA safety official, she lives and writes in the beautiful Shenandoah Valley of Virginia. A graduate of Madison College (now James Madison University), she has degrees in history and political science. Politics and history manage to work their way into her writing.

She is president of the Virginia Writers Club, one of the oldest writer organizations in the country.

Her fiction has appeared in numerous literary journals and anthologies. When not writing, reading, reviewing books, singing in a UU choir, watching the Yankees, or cheering on Dale Earnhardt, Jr., she delights in spoiling her grandchildren.

SOCIAL MEDIA

TWITTER: @unspywriter
FACEBOOK AUTHOR PAGE:
    https://www.facebook.com/unspywriter
BLOG: www.unexpectedpaths.com
INSTAGRAM: paduncan1
AMAZON AUTHOR PAGE: (links to published work)
    http://bit.ly/PADuncan

ALSO BY THE AUTHOR

SHORT STORY/FLASH FICTION COLLECTIONS:

Rarely Well-Behaved, 2000 (out of print)
Blood Vengeance, 2012
Fences and Other Stories, 2012

www.ingramcontent.com/pod-product-compliance
Lightning Source LLC
Chambersburg PA
CBHW060935120626
46557CB00003B/997